SILLY INSANE HUMANS

BOOK 3: The Robot
Galaxy Series

Adeena Mignogna

SILLY INSANE HUMANS

ISBN: 979-8-9855963-1-1 (paperback)

Edited by: Carolani Bartell

Book cover design by: Ebooklaunch.com

Published by Crazy Robot, LLC

(** except for the name/character Patrick Marsden. I know a Patrick Marsden in real life, and he said I could use his name for a character one day when I was stuck for a name and asked all my Facebook friends whose name I could use. Pat volunteered.)

The Robot Galaxy Series

Book 1: Crazy Foolish Robots

Book 2: Robots, Robots Everywhere!

Book 3: Silly Insane Humans

Book 4: Eleven Little Robots

DEDICATION

To all the Umans I've ever encountered or been inspired by: simple and complex; sensible and rational; insane and lucid.

Before We Begin

'Are we alone in the Universe?' has been one of the greatest unanswered questions of all time. It is right up there with other important unanswered questions such as 'Why do so many people hate licorice?' and 'Why does the number of cats a person collects increase proportionally with the length of time they've been socially isolated as well as to their hoarding status?'

Over the years, all the great minds of science—and science fiction—have been asked to speculate on the status of not only whether or not aliens exist but what they were like, where they were located, and when and how first contact would occur.

Not a single human who lived on Earth, one of Earth's colonies, or one of the human-made space stations envisioned that first contact would be with a group of alien robots. (With the exception of one obscure science fiction writer who published works in the early 21st century.)

Yet, many humans had looked to the stars with all manner of increasingly fancy technology to try and see if they could find evidence of life.

As of the year 2192, they had not. All of this changed on a regular Tuesday in 2192 when humankind received a message. The message was from one of their own, Ruby Palmer, a nineteen-year-old, who had been presumed dead for the last week and for the two weeks prior to that, known to be missing.

But on this Saturday, in a message intended for her uncles, on the space station Astroll 2, where she had lived since the age of seven, she declared to every human who was at that moment in front of a screen that she had spent the last several weeks in the company of robots. Alien robots.

On the other hand, these robots had been well aware for quite some time now that a multitude of biological life forms inhabited the galaxy.

Their opinions of Bios, as they not-so-lovingly called them, were that they typically did not seem to have a well-constructed program to execute, and hence, it was hard to predict what kinds of actions they would take. Not to mention all the processes they executed in order to continue functioning were, for lack of a better term, messy.

The robots followed their programming as provided to them through the various agencies and Halls that made up the Core of their society.

But there was a 'Special Projects' department responsible for ensuring that a set of robots had programming related to finding their long-lost data storage.

Detailed Historian, known as Disto, was one robot who received this programming and had been on a mission to collect and test the DNA of various biological life to determine whose DNA was used as a storage mechanism.

The robots had one main unanswered question that plagued them: 'Who created us?' The difference between a robot asking that and a human was that the robots knew an answer existed and that it was likely tucked away in their long-lost data archive.

Ruby Palmer, who had been with the robots for a few weeks, had her DNA tested and it was determined that humans did not carry any of the robots' data in the section of their DNA that was 'junk' to humankind.

But Ruby explained that there were thousands of other species of animals on planet Earth, so maybe one of those were what they were looking for. Maybe more than one.

So, Disto agreed to accompany Ruby Palmer back to her home. Swell Driver, known as SD, and the robot that first whisked Ruby away to Location Zero, the robot's home planet, was driving the ship. They were further accompanied by Ambitious Technician, AT, who simply wanted his adventure to continue.

In addition to being well aware of the common questions they shared as a conglomerate, each had their own questions they wanted answered.

AT wanted to know 'what kind of things will I be able to fix? Will I be able to learn their new technology?"

Disto only had thoughts about testing DNA. He wondered how long it was going to take to test all of the various types of Bios on this planet. Ruby didn't have an exact count but believed a couple million different species were left. Disto nearly had a circuit pop when he heard that number. While they had quite a bit of information on her home world, Planet Earth, the number of species in the robots' database cut off somewhat arbitrarily at 4068. Even that was quite a number.

SD's question wasn't quite so specific, however. SD was working hard to not let his question surface to his working memory: 'what is wrong with me?' A question to which he had no idea where to begin.

And finally, Ruby had only one question on her mind: "How mad are my uncles going to be?" given she had run away, stolen a ship, and was bringing it back in pieces.

Chapter 1

> Ruby <

Ruby entered the command center of SD's ship. It looked as it had when she was first here—roomy for a single robot and human, sparse, with a single console indicating where a pilot might stand, and that was the spot SD occupied as he had that first day. She had previously been examining the parts of her own mini-R-pod, *Apple Pi*, as it lay strewn about in the belly of SD's ship.

"We are approaching the heliopause," SD announced.

"What is that?" AT asked. Ruby had come to learn in the short week she had known AT that he was very much the technician his name implied. If it wasn't related to something he could work on or fix, his knowledge was not only limited but practically non-existent.

To that end, they had to explain space travel to him. He knew the concept existed but didn't know how it worked. He had never worked on or fixed a spaceship before. In the sector of Location Zero that AT was from, they didn't have any outgoing or incoming ships.

But to prep for this trip, AT downloaded all the specs and diagrams, so he'd be prepared in case he needed to fix something.

In the short journey, nothing needed to be fixed, so AT

occupied his time asking a large quantity of questions regarding anything space travel related.

"It's considered the boundary of our solar system," Ruby said. She was, in fact, well-versed in all things related to space travel, even ones that had been considered out of bounds. Her mini-R-pod, *Apple Pi*, was designed only for relatively short-range travel. Its general range was from her home on the Astroll 2 space station to various other asteroids in the asteroid belt. In a pinch, it could take someone a few million kilometers away. For example, to Titan, one of the moons of Saturn and her original destination when she had left Astroll 2 shortly before SD found her.

Ruby was pacing as she answered AT's question. The nervous pacing prompted her to spew out everything she knew on the concept: "It's a theoretical boundary, not one any human has passed through. A few space probes have gone further, so I guess we know a little bit about it. It's where the solar wind and the interstellar medium meet."

"What is the solar wind?" AT asked.

Ruby shook her head. "Can I just give you a textbook to read? I can't handle all these questions right now."

Disto looked up from the computer console he had been engrossed in studying.

"Are you okay, Ruby?" he asked.

Ruby appreciated that Disto was able to ask her questions like that. At the right time, too. Thinking back to when they first met and how Disto was completely unaware, or didn't care, or was utterly perplexed by her emotional state, Ruby was grateful for the robot's attempts at meeting her halfway. She gave a little and they did too.

"I'm just nervous," Ruby said. "I wish I knew that my uncles got my message. I have no idea what they're going to say."

"Fearless Communicator assured us that his method to deliver your message was guaranteed not to fail."

"I know. Then assume they got it. I just told them that I'm with a bunch of alien robots. What are they thinking?"

"You will be able to ask them shortly," SD interrupted. "Please look." SD pointed to the screen which was so large, Ruby envied it. It was mostly black, and there were several dots, ranging from tiny to large but not large enough to be anything other than a dot. Each dot that had some importance were bracketed by square braces, and a symbol appeared below.

"Are those…" Ruby began.

"Those are the planets of your solar system along with our default designations. Here, I will turn on the predicted orbits of them."

Faint, but visible dotted lines appeared. From that, Ruby was able to see that the largest dot was really the Sun. She counted. All 8 planets were accounted for. A couple of the dwarf planets, too.

"Nice," she said. "But where's Astroll 2?"

Astroll 2 was located in the asteroid belt, near the Dwarf Planet Ceres. Ceres had been the source of a lot of contention to corporations and governments back on Earth over the years. As such, it was a designated 'do not touch' dwarf planet. As far as Ruby knew, everyone abided by that. So, the company that built, owned, and operated Astroll 2 mined other nearby asteroids.

Over the years, there had been on and off plans for another active station, but none had popped up. Astroll 2, and its nearly 2,000 inhabitants, was the key facility in that region of space.

SD tapped his console, and another marker appeared on the screen. Given its location, Ruby clearly identified it as Astroll 2. They were close. Not close enough that *Apple Pi*, if it had been in the condition to fly, could get her there, but close in the sense that they were in the same solar system and not 54 light years away.

"Do you want to fly by any of the planets or moons on our way there?" SD asked. "I can program a variety of trajectories through the system."

Ruby considered that. She was already the first human to meet an extraterrestrial—unless ancient alien abduction stories could be believed. Right now, she couldn't be certain either way. As far as she knew, she was the first human ever to leave the solar system. Why not be the first to see all the planets up close?

"Sure," she said. She knew deep down that what she was doing was, in fact, procrastinating from making contact with her family on Astroll 2.

Chapter 2

> Swell Driver <

While his companions talked about all the phenomena out there in the Universe, specifically in Ruby's home system, Swell Driver was free to think about whatever he wanted while he computed a trajectory that would take them on a tour of Ruby's solar system.

He heard Ruby tell stories of the various planets, from the large to the small, gaseous to rocky. While she talked, SD ruminated on himself.

SD called up the memories from the last time he was here. It was the last time he could recall feeling like himself.

He used an appendage to plug into his computer console. That was the polite thing to do when others were around.

He remembered passing through a storm of radiation on his way here, which corrupted much of the data in his ship's systems. But no, that wasn't the problem. He still felt fine and himself.

SD could recall a time not too long ago when the computer told him that Ruby's kind were called 'Umans' and provided him the misinformation that they looked entirely different from Ruby. And he could recall that his primary algorithm, which involved piloting spaceships to ferry things across the galaxy, was intact then. It was intact now.

"How far are we from initiating tour of the Bio-Muck

system," SD asked the ship's computer. While Ruby had helped SD relabel much of the data he had on her system, planet, and its contents, the name for the overall system hadn't changed.

"Less than 66 tics if we start now," the computer responded.

"Wonderful. Set for autonomous…"

"But there are several ships in the path between the fourth planet and the construction known as Astroll 2."

"Interesting. Adjust course to take us…"

"And I can detect several locations that are scanning Astroll 2 and its vicinity. We will pass through those scanners."

"*Very* interesting. We will adjust the trajectory to avoid that."

SD instructed the computer to head along a trajectory that would take them parallel to the axis of spin of the majority of the planets, thus putting them at a vantage point that most would consider 'overhead' of the system. They would weave in and out by going 'up and down' from most lifeforms' vantage point. Only the lifeforms in this system should not be expecting that, and hence wouldn't detect them.

Not that a detection would be terrible in this case. They were going to make contact with Ruby's relatives. This thought excited SD. Ruby was swell, and after all the stories she'd told about her uncles, cousin, and even her friends, figured they would all be swell, too.

"233 tics until new trajectory can be initiated," the computer told SD.

"Excellent. Set for autonomous execution," SD ordered the computer.

To his companions, he said, "Would you like to see a live feed of each item as we pass by?"

"Yes, of course!" said Ruby. She disengaged from whatever she was talking about to Disto and AT and came over to SD's side, putting a hand on his chassis. He was always comforted when she did that. That's how Ruby would describe the feeling anyway. SD would use a more specific term such as, 'certain,' perhaps, or 'secure.' Certain that someone he enjoyed was nearby and secure in the fact that they weren't going anywhere.

SD set the viewscreen to display live feeds of whatever entity they were approaching. A small spherical object appeared and started to grow in the screen.

"That's Pluto!" Ruby said. "Everyone's favorite not-quite-a-planet planet."

"What does that mean?" Disto asked.

"It used to be a planet, but then it became a Dwarf Planet," said Ruby.

"How does a planet undergo such a transformation?"

Ruby giggled. "It didn't," she said. "It was just a change in nomenclature."

"Ah," all three robots said in unison.

"Yeah, it caused a big kerfuffle at the time. I read about it in a class I had to take on the history of the solar system. Apparently, people who had barely ever heard of Pluto came out of the woodwork to defend it as a planet."

"Woodwork?" SD asked. He was used to asking Ruby about some of the odd phrases she used.

"It means that people who didn't care before all of the sudden cared."

"Why?" asked AT.

"I have no idea," said Ruby. "They just did. It took forty or so years for it to settle out. I think I have a great-great-great-great-great grandmother who might have been involved in helping people to accept it. I can't remember her name, but she would try and tell people the positive side of the situation. It got people to learn more about the dwarf planets, which apparently no one knew about before all of that."

"Does anyone live there?" Disto asked.

"Oh no," said Ruby. "In fact, I think I'm the closest any human has ever come to seeing it up close like this. It's beautiful!"

"Beautiful?" all three robots repeated in unison.

SD was starting to look up the definition of that word, but Disto was a little faster. He added, "pleasing the circuits and algorithms.''

Ruby's face contorted in a way that made SD wonder if that was indeed the definition, but then she returned to watching the object she called 'Pluto' on the screen. Their trajectory had them encircle the planet at approximately three times its diameter before heading further inwards towards the next planet on the tour, one Ruby called 'Uranus.' They were not going to pass by all the planets 'in order' of their distance from the Sun, but rather along a path that aligned with the planet's current positions.

SD and the other robots were quiet for a moment and watched Ruby watching Pluto. SD identified his feeling as pity in that moment. He understood that Human spaceships were quite limited, and as such, this type of tour of their own solar system, their home, was impossible. Ruby, who was even a pilot like himself, had so little experience flying compared to him. He knew that she would love to pilot this ship herself if she could.

He wished that was something he could allow her to do. It was a wish that had been developing in his circuits for a while but there were still competing algorithms that computed that only he could pilot his ship. Once again, he began ruminating on his own failings as a robot, a habit that Explosive Healer had tried to break in him during their sessions together before she was destroyed. Explosive Healer tried to tell him that the things happening to and around him were not his fault. SD tried to incorporate her counsel into his algorithms, and the computational result was believing that if he executed his assignments, like a good robot, he'd get to do what he wanted afterwards. Although he wasn't even sure he could compute what he wanted accurately…

Chapter 3

> Ruby <

"That was amazing," Ruby said. "I have no words for the gift you've just given me." The magnitude of what she just did, become the first human to see all eight planets and a handful of dwarf planets up close, was settling in.

Saturn, with its moon Titan, along with Jupiter, had always been her favorites, especially since Titan was where she longed to be for the longest time. But seeing Earth up close, yet not too close, gave her a tingly feeling that tugged at her a little. She wasn't going to admit out loud that it might have supplanted the others as her new favorite, but she appreciated its beauty when you couldn't see what was happening on the surface.

"And really, it's all recorded?" she asked.

SD nodded. "Yes. We'll be able to provide you with an assemblage of the data."

She was the first human to see the entire solar system up close, *and* she was going to be able to bring a record of the experience back with her. SD had told her that not only was she seeing things in a visual spectrum suited to her, but the ship had the capability to record all the way from low-frequency radio waves to gamma rays—pretty much covering the entire electromagnetic spectrum. That data would keep a handful of scientists busy for their entire careers.

Humans had colonized Mars and knew that planet pretty well, and also knew a few things about Titan and the couple of other places humans had been. Support for exploring the system, specifically the parts that would probably never be lived on, touched by humans, or made any use of, had waned over the years. It was hot and heavy in the early 21st century, but enough people complained about the amount of money being spent off of Earth that by 2050, there was nothing happening. The Mars colony was left over from the early days of human space exploration. Anything else that existed with a human footprint was purely the result of the trillionaires—they created The Company and started ZTEC, the organization that was only recently starting to explore Titan.

Ruby had tried to learn everything she could about Titan, including old history—several missions had been planned in the early 21st century, but none of them materialized.

"We have one more object to see on our current trajectory," SD said. "We're headed to Ceres before we approach Astroll 2."

Ruby gulped. The moment she had been anxious about was upon her.

"How long until we start our Astroll 2 approach?" she asked.

"Approximately six hundred and, no, calculating… ten minutes."

Ruby smiled softly. She appreciated how the robots were attempting to talk in terms of the human time scale now that they were in her home system. On Location Zero, it made sense that they referred to any unit of time in their own scale, the tic, which was nearly one second. But it was nice that they were adjusting while here.

She was stalling from thinking about what she was going to say to her uncles.

As if the robots could read her thoughts, Disto said, "And approximately five minutes until we are able to initiate a communication channel."

Ruby gulped again.

"How do I look?" she said to no robot in particular. All three of the robots looked at each other and back to Ruby, and then back to each other.

"You look like your systems are functioning normally," AT said.

"You look the same as the day I... met you," said SD.

"The hue of your outer chassis is a slightly different hue from what is typical," Disto said, "but I think you look... fine."

Ruby appreciated Disto's attention to language. In truth, she appreciated all the interactions she had with these robots up until now. After getting off to a rough start initially—after all, they did kidnap her—they were genuinely kind and took care of all her needs. They provided her interesting information about their planet and society. And, of course, their manner of speaking, at least how they processed her language and idioms, provided no end of entertainment.

And she was taking them home to meet her family.

"Has it been five minutes?" she asked, more because no one else had said anything, and she wanted to hear someone talk.

"Indeed," Disto said. "Let's try to establish communication. AT?"

AT had plugged himself into the console. Ruby had provided him with information earlier on the various communication frequencies that were used—including which ones to avoid since they were for emergency purposes only.

Ruby stood in front of one of the console screens, which came to life almost immediately. The face that greeted her was... she was trying to remember where she had seen him before.

It was the FUFE who tried to help, or rather, didn't really try, but sent her to call the main care center on Earth the day she left Astroll 2.

At first, he was not looking at the screen, but seemingly at another console on his end and his expression was one of indifference as he talked from a script he had memorized, "We're here to take care of you, if we don't then..." as he looked at the screen that would have been showing him Ruby's face, "holy amaze-balls! You're Ruby Palmer! Just one moment!"

Ruby searched her memory but couldn't recall this guy knowing who she was the last time they interacted. She also couldn't imagine why she would spark such a reaction.

"Ok," he said after a moment of furious tapping on another device. "Robt Plampton is in his office, and your uncle, I don't know which one, is on his way there. I'm going to route this call to the Director's office. Stand by. Wow! Ruby Palmer! I'd love to have dinner with you later and you can tell me all about—"

He was cut off and his image was replaced by the current director of Astroll 2, Robt Plampton. Plampton's face was round, in a way that someone who had spent nearly their entire adult life in space, mostly in the very low-gravity of ships, would look. His complexion, not pale, but not sun-kissed, also betrayed a life in artificial environments. His pug nose and large ears were not features that commanded respect, but his blue eyes worked over-time on that.

Those were the same eyes that went wide when he saw Ruby.

"Ruby Palmer! It is you! This is amazing!"

Ruby was not sure what to say. This over-the-top reaction was not what she was expecting.

"Hi, Mr. Plampton," she said, a little uncertain. "I really wanted to talk to my uncles. Are they there?"

"Blake is on his way," Plampton said. He then looked around Ruby, moving awkwardly back and forth as one might while seeing something unbelievable displayed on a flat screen. As if he was struggling to accept the 2D image and needed to force perspective into it being 3D.

"Are they with you now?" he said.

"Wha… who?" Ruby looked over to her left at one robot and two others over on her right. *He couldn't mean…* but before she had time to continue that awkward questioning, she saw a door swish open behind Robt Plampton and Uncle Blake appeared.

He quickly replaced Plampton in the viewscreen as he moved Robt Plampton over to the side. Plampton was still ogling at every angle of Ruby's image as he could manage.

"Uncle Blake!" Ruby felt like she was going to melt. "I am so happy to see you! I can't wait to tell you! Wait… you got my message? You knew I was okay? And you shared my message with Mr. Plampton?" Ruby was finally catching on. That had to be it. Plampton knew about the robots, too. That would make sense. If it were a normal day, she might've caught on sooner. But Ruby hadn't had a normal day since she was last onboard Astroll 2. The amount of new information and experiences she'd been taking in were beginning to feel entirely unmanageable. She had taken a mini-R-pod, so when her uncles got her message, they probably felt obligated to tell the station director.

"Your message was shared, but *I* wasn't the one who shared it. But, Ruby, oh, I'm so glad to see you!" Uncle Blake said.

"Wait a minute. Other people saw my message? That was just for you and Uncle Logan."

"Ruby, it wasn't only *some* people who saw your message. *Everyone* in the whole solar system got it. You're, well, famous. Let's get you back on Astroll 2, and I'll explain everything that's been happening since the MCE—the Moment that Changed Everything."

Chapter 4

> Milo <

Milo's heart was racing.

"How can I help you calm down?" his communicuff offered.

"Delete notification," Milo said. He was in the hanger prepping a mini-R-pod, *Pecan Pi*, for launch. It was bad enough that his communicuff knew how fast his heart was racing. He didn't need his team to know as well.

But he admitted to himself that his heart was only half racing because he was going to see Ruby again. The other half was about that alien ship holding position a few hundred kilometers from Astroll 2.

The ship was huge, larger than anything he'd ever worked on. It was larger than anything in any human ship fleet he was even aware of. As such, it was too big to fit in either hanger of Astroll 2.

Apparently, Ruby's ship, *Apple Pi*, was inside it, but it was not functioning, so it couldn't bring Ruby back to Astroll 2. Instead, it was decided, as he was informed by Robt Plampton, that he, Milo Jenkins, would take another mini-R-pod out, dock with the alien ship, and bring Ruby home.

Not just Ruby. Three alien robots were going to accompany her. He was still having trouble fathoming such a thing.

"I have multiple strategies," his communicuff chimed again,

"to help you reduce your heart rate. It is not healthy to maintain such a high resting heart rate."

"Delete notification," Milo instructed again. "Discontinue heart rate monitoring until further notice."

"That is not recommended. Fourteen out of fifteen human and AI doctors recommend—"

"Delete."

Milo looked around the mini-R-pod. Two members of his team were on the opposite side inspecting the phalanges. A do-nothing part, but every ship that carried humans had at least one or two. There was a law enacted in 2091 that stated every ship must have phalanges and the number was proportional to the number of people the ship could support. This mini-R-pod had two. Milo was now in a long line of technicians and other industry professionals who simply shook their heads, inspected the phalanges, and moved on with life.

Pecan Pi was the largest. It was actually a mini-R-pod-L. It was slightly bigger than Ruby's *Apple Pi*, and Milo was assured that it would fit into the alien ship parked outside.

He felt his heart rate pick up speed once again at the thought. This time, his communicuff remained silent.

Milo looked at the tablet he had been carrying around. He reviewed the pre-launch checklist that was displayed.

"Hey, Domas, your part of the inspection complete?" As the words came out of his mouth, he saw that several steps in the procedure took on a green highlight. "Never mind," he called out and walked around the ship, giving it a final glance.

"Ready to go rescue your *girlfriend?*" Domas Watkins snickered. His companion, Eryk Chung snickered as well.

Milo, never one who appreciated that kind of joking around, said, "Two things wrong with your statement. One, she's not my girlfriend. I have a date with Inny later, remember? Two, I'm not rescuing her. She's fine. Just doesn't have a way to get back onto the station."

"Fine, fine, she's not your girlfriend," Domas conceded. Although mentioning his date with Innogen gave Milo a sick feeling in his stomach. It was a date, but it wasn't. Sure, since

Ruby's disappearance, they had become closer. Closer *friends*. Still, she called it a date, and he hadn't disagreed. He tried to, but it came out as an odd assortment of stuttering 'ums,' and 'ers.' Inny asked him what was wrong, and he proceeded to shovel a much-too-large portion of his calci-cinna roll into his mouth to keep himself from saying something stupid.

"But," Domas said as Milo opened the hatch to *Pecan Pi*, "I mean, she's with aliens. Alien robots. How creepy-cool!"

"There's a rumor going around that they're coming back with you, too," Eryk said.

"Well, that's a rumor you should keep to yourself," Milo responded. Director Plampton had indeed told him not to mention that. There were a lot of mixed feelings about alien robots coming to the station, and Plampton didn't want things to get out of hand. He said he wanted to make sure they debriefed Ruby—and the robots—properly before it was well known.

Milo didn't know how that would happen without creating more suspicion. Once he returned to the hanger, his whole team would know. And if four people knew something interesting, the whole station of 2,000 would, too, shortly after. Oh well, it was a noble goal on Plampton's part, and he wouldn't add fuel to that fire, but he wasn't going to be able to prevent anything.

"It sounds like they're perfectly nice. Ruby said she was well taken care of," Milo said, hoping to ease any fears.

"You talked to her?"

"No," Milo admitted, "Plampton told me."

"And you believe him?"

"No reason not to," Milo responded. "Now, let's get me out into space." He walked into the ship and closed the hatch behind him. Since this was the shortest trip ever planned, he took nothing except the tablet he had been holding which he now stowed in a compartment over the second pilot's console.

Through the cockpit window he saw his team head back to the control center and before he knew it, he was in space and on a heading to rendezvous with an alien ship.

He had taken an extra sweat-suppression pill before leaving his quarters earlier, and wished he'd brought a third pill since the next few minutes had the ability to leave him drenched in nervous sweat—something he wasn't anxious for Ruby, or anyone, to see.

> Milo <

Before this moment, Astroll 2 was the largest manufactured object Milo had ever seen in space. But the ship parked in front of him, which looked like it came right out of an old, animated children's movie, was nearly half the size of Astroll 2. Larger than any ship he'd ever seen or read about.

The ship was stationary, at least with respect to Astroll 2, which was good. But without a place to attach himself, he figured the best he could do was to put himself in a circumnavigational path around the ship.

This had the extra benefit of allowing him a good look at the thing. Besides being huge, the other word he'd used to describe it was whale-like. It was boxy, but there was a clear seam where a whale's mouth would be. He couldn't make out any windows, nor determine where thrust would expel to move the ship. None of the features that he recognized on human-made ships seemed to present itself on this… blob. His brain was back to large and boxy but whale shaped. Perhaps it was this that made him feel as if he was about to be swallowed whole.

"Computer, are you recording the object in front of us?"

"Confirmed. Ship's cameras are recording."

"Are we in danger of running out of data storage space?"

"Storage is at 5.3% and increasing at a rate of 0.1% per minute."

Once Milo determined that his orbit around the monster ship was stable, he initiated a communication link. Well, he turned on his communication link and hoped that it was one that the alien ship could receive.

"This is *Pecan Pi* calling…" he wasn't sure what he was

calling. Standard greeting was to identify the other ship, but he hadn't been given a name. "This is *Pecan Pi* calling the alien ship." He closed his eyes and squished them. He sounded like a dorky kid from one of those animated movies. He was starting to think that he was part of one. Or maybe this was a dream.

"What's cooking, *Pecan Pi?*" Milo heard a familiar voice but would have sworn on his entire meme archive there was a high-pitched crack on the word 'what.'

"Ruby!"

"Hi, Milo. Come to rescue me and bring me home?" Ruby said with a chuckle. Milo didn't know what the chuckle was. Was she flirting with him? No, that couldn't be. If he chuckled back, would she think that he was flirting with her? Milo definitely didn't want that. But she chuckled, so maybe if he didn't, she would think something was wrong and wouldn't feel welcomed.

Milo attempted a subtle chuckle that turned into a wheeze and a throat clearing, "I'm going to try! What's the plan? How do I get you out of that thing?"

There was a pause, and then Ruby said, "Cut your thruster power, try to minimize any remaining thrust. SD says once your momentum is at a minimum, we'll," there was another pause, "we'll scoop you up. Easy peasy."

Milo blinked. "SD?"

"Yeah, that's the name of, uh, one of my new friends. You'll meet him in just a few minutes. Drop that momentum, ok?"

"Understood," Milo said and then went to work on his console applying specific impulses to the different maneuvering thrusters all over *Pecan Pi* until he was as still as he could be relative to the alien ship.

He looked out the window. The ship started to rotate until the mouth of the whale was facing him. Then it opened up and enveloped his ship.

Chapter 5

> Detailed Historian <

Detailed Historian looked at the tiny ship sent to retrieve Ruby.

"We will all fit in there?" he asked, uncertain as his circuits made some geometrical estimations based on what his optical sensors could perceive.

"Sure," Ruby said. "We'll be cozy, but it's not like it's a week-long trip. It'll take us only a few minutes to get to Astroll 2 from here. We'll be fine."

Disto, as he thought of himself ever since working out his preferred nickname, wasn't so sure, and wanted to ask if there were other options. He wanted to but decided to say nothing, only because audio communication with Bios was typically slow and introduced so much delay in whatever was happening, and he was anxious to get on with things.

He was not only anxious to get to Astroll 2, but anxious to get to Ruby's home planet, Earth. That's where millions of biological species were located, any one of which could be the link to the robot's long-lost storage data.

Several generations ago, robots had used the junk DNA of some alien species as storage, as their world was facing a storage crisis. It wasn't Ruby's species, the humans, but their planet had more life than was typical of any other biological species they'd ever met, so it was highly likely that one, or more, of the species of her home planet was exactly what he was looking for. The sooner he could start examining all that DNA, the more content a robot he would be.

Ruby told him she wasn't sure when or how they would get back to Earth, but that they certainly would. There were some biological samples on Astroll 2, however, that they could ask for him to look at in the meantime.

"Generally, animals haven't been welcome in space," she had said. "A few are used in experiments, but that's it."

"Not welcome?"

"Ok, bad choice of words. They take up too many resources that humans use and need. I once overheard an argument one of the hanger chiefs had with someone who had snuck their pet cat aboard. They were arguing with the station director about how they needed it. I don't think either of them stayed on Astroll 2."

Ruby, while very useful when it came to all things computers and programming—after all, she had helped his kind with a couple of major problems—was not useful at all when it came to discussing the myriad of life on her home world.

Maybe it was because she had lived most of her life away from it, on the station she called Astroll 2. Maybe it was because she was too focused all the time on her own interests that everything else was a blur. Or maybe it was simply that her own programming was limited.

Disto then felt a small jolt. He recognized that it must be the scooping hatch securing in its closed state.

"Capture complete," SD announced.

"Ok! Milo is probably freaking out right about now, I know I was," Ruby said. "Let me see and talk to him first, okay?"

Disto approximated a nod to show agreement and saw both SD and AT make a similar motion.

They all moved to the lift at the back of the cabin. Moments later, they were in front of a small ship.

"Give it a sec for the temperature to even out," Ruby said. "We let the outermost part of the hull get cold. It's part of the thermal design to keep the inside a good temperature for us humans without using too much power."

"How long does that take?" asked AT. "I would love to know more about how your transportation vessels work. Maybe I can help you finish putting together your ship."

Disto looked over at the partially assembled, but mostly disassembled, *Apple Pi*, the ship that Ruby had been in when SD met her.

"Let me see," and Disto watched her take the end of her appendage and touch the ship. She immediately pulled it back but said, "Eh, we can open it. It's fine."

She then used the same appendage to release a clamp on the side of a hatch, which swung down.

"Hey Milo!" she called into the ship. "You in there?"

There was no response.

"Milo?" Ruby rushed into the ship. And then, a moment later, Disto heard, "I need some help!"

Disto rushed into the ship, followed by AT.

He saw Ruby trying to move another Bio, who was slumped over the console, back into his chair. AT came over and helped with the maneuvering.

"He has a normal pulse," she said, adding, "I think."

"Milo, talk to me. Wake up?" Ruby was tapping his cheek. "I need the emergency med kit. AT, can you open that drawer?"

She was pointing to one right behind where Disto was standing, so he turned around and used his own appendage to open it.

"Yeah, that's the one. There's a red box…"

Disto didn't know what red was but saw two boxes. He pulled them both out, but before he could give either to Ruby, the new Bio made a noise. It wasn't a word that was in his dictionary of the Ruby's language. It was, "uuuugghh."

"Milo! You're ok!" Ruby said and sat in the chair next to him.

The other Bio, apparently designated 'Milo,' brought his appendages to the top of his chassis and rubbed them around his optical sensors.

24

"Yeah, I uh... I think I passed out."

Ruby laughed. "Yeah, you did! Wait until I tell—"

"Oh, please don't," Milo said.

"Milo, it's so good to see you," Ruby said and wrapped her appendages around him. Disto was certain that he sensed some kind of change in Milo based upon Ruby's action, but wasn't sure what or why. "Let me introduce you to my, uh, new friends."

"They're here?" Milo said.

"They're right behind you."

Disto watched as Milo turned in his direction. His optical sensors were wide, and Disto could tell that Milo was scanning him.

"That's a, uh," Milo stood up and was attempting to move backwards into the console. Disto couldn't understand that movement since there was equipment blocking his way.

"Yeah," Ruby said, "it's a robot. Actually, they're all robots."

Disto watched as Milo realized that AT was much closer to him and tried to move further back, all while performing the same scanning procedure on AT.

"Milo, this is Ambitious Technician, who we call 'AT'. AT, meet Milo."

"Greetings, Milo," said AT. Milo just shook his head.

"And this is Detailed Historian, also known as Disto," Ruby gestured in his own direction. "Disto, meet Milo Jenkins. He's a friend and one of the hanger chiefs on the station."

"Nice to meet you, Milo Jenkins," Disto said. Milo again nodded and his tense body seemed to relax.

"Ruby," Disto said, "Does Milo Jenkins have an alias as well?"

"I don't know," Ruby responded, "Milo, do you? I've always called him Milo."

"A what?" Milo said.

"A nickname. Do you have a nickname?"

Milo moved his head back and forth. Disto understood that human gesture meant negative.

"And you must meet SD, the driver of our ship. Where is he?" Disto looked around. SD clearly hadn't followed them into Milo's ship. He went back out the hatch and saw SD perched in front of it.

"SD, are you not traveling with us?"

SD didn't move. His circuits were active, however. Disto could tell that by the wavy coloring SD's chassis produced.

"SD?"

It was as if SD exited a programming loop.

"I must prep the ship if we are all going to leave," he said and went back up the lift.

Disto returned to the small ship and said to Ruby, "SD needs a few minutes to prepare. Then we'll all be ready to go."

"When Plampton said that the robots would be coming back, I…" Milo trailed off.

Ruby smiled at him and patted his chassis with her appendage. "They're awesome once you get to know them." Then she looked at Disto.

"Disto," Ruby said, "you can put those back."

He hadn't realized he still held the two small boxes she had asked for moments ago. He replaced them in their drawer and said, "As you wish."

SD appeared and announced, "I have set the ship to standby mode. We can leave anytime." Then to a dangling green fractal construction that was inset into one of the wall panels, "Oh look, this ship has one of those objects as well. Ruby, do you remember when I mistook this for a human?"

Ruby chuckled. "Yes, and do you remember how freaked out I was?"

"Is that the reaction that Milo is experiencing?" Disto asked.

Everyone turned to look at the new human in the room.

Ruby, still sitting in the seat next to Milo said, "Yes, but I was definitely more freaked out. Remember, I had no idea about any of you. Milo at least had a clue. Right, Milo?"

"Ruby," Milo said sternly, "*everyone* has a clue."

Ruby scrunched her face. "Um. Uncle Blake said something

like that, too. I don't quite understand. What am I missing?"

Disto was glad that question wasn't aimed at him, since he detected that she was complete with one-hundred-percent of her parts where they should be. She was missing nothing he could observe. He wouldn't have known how to answer the question.

"Let's get ready to depart and I'll tell you about my MCE," Milo said.

"MCE?" Ruby asked. "I think that's what Uncle Blake called it, too." Disto saw her furrowed brow and wanted to ask her about it but stored his questions for later.

Disto marveled at the differences between the two Bios. They obviously came from the same species, but beyond that, there were more differences than he could count. They evidently didn't come from the same template. But neither did he and SD or he and AT. Therefore, he shouldn't have been surprised. He wasn't surprised, exactly, but interested.

He listened while the two humans prepared the small ship for departure. There was nothing for him, or the other two robots, to do. Disto could tell that made both SD and AT anxious. Neither was the kind of robot who liked to sit and do nothing.

Less than a click later, they were out in space and nearly at Astroll 2.

Chapter 6

> Ruby <

There was a welcome party in the hanger. She could see through the window that a whole group of people were gathered in the cramped space of the hanger control room, not simply the hanger team.

"Milo, it looks like half the station is crammed in there," she said.

"Ruby, I'm not sure you get it yet. You're famous. Like, mega famous. Like, I'm not worthy to be talking to you kind of famous."

"Because of the MCE?" she asked.

"Exactly," said Milo. "Everyone remembers every detail about where they were and what they were doing when they saw your message about being with those robots." He aimed his thumb over his shoulder at the robots, who were also all looking out the window.

Ruby smirked with her mouth pursed tight and let one eyebrow go up. "Oh, c'mon. That's ridiculous. Even if that's even a little true, that's ridiculous." As the word ridiculous rolled off her tongue, her eye was drawn to someone in the hanger, standing close to the window who was wearing a t-shirt that had… her face! And big, bold text that read, "I'm with robots!"

"Ruby. We thought you were dead. And then you're not

dead, and you're with aliens. Extraterrestrials. This is…," Ruby watched Milo look at the robots behind them while they waited for the hanger crew to close the hanger door and ensure the hanger was returned to the right oxygen and pressure levels. It usually took a few minutes, and there was nothing to do in this time but wait in one's ship.

There was actually a procedure she would do to stow everything if this had been a normal flight. But this had not.

"You guys okay back there?" she said to the robots, trying to center herself more than anything. She was with robots, after all.

"Indeed," called Disto. "I am admiring the welcome party."

"Yeah, me too," Ruby said, although 'admiring' was definitely not the right word. But the people she wanted to see most in the galaxy were there: her uncles. She didn't see Sebastian, her seven-year-old cousin, but that wasn't too surprising. She had checked station time and it was the middle of the night.

And then she remembered…

"Oh! Milo! The mini-R-pods! Have they had the AI upgrade yet?"

"No, not yet. We got some kind of cryptic message from The Company that told us to hold off. They didn't tell us why. I'm sure it was some minor bug or a patch they wanted to apply."

Ruby let out a breath. "Oh good," she said. Then, "'Bug' my butt. I had some time on Location Zero to—"

"Location Zero?" Milo interrupted.

"Yeah, that's what the robots call their home planet."

"Very… exotic," Milo smirked.

"Sure, but listen to me. While there, I was able to test out the mini-R-pod upgrade. Remember that *Apple Pi* had it staged. Well, I transferred it to my MoDaC…"

"The same *Apple Pi* that's sitting in pieces in that… that ship?"

"Stop interrupting me and let me tell my story! This is important!"

Milo put his hands up, indicating she could continue.

"Ok—I'll skip to the end. There's a bug in there, alright. A *big* one! It's expecting to pick up on the location services that can only be accessed in the Earth-Mars network. Beyond Mars, it just won't work!"

She watched as Milo's face cycled through a series of expressions, processing what she had just told him.

"Well, they said there was a bug. Are you sure that's what it is?" Milo asked.

"Absolutely," Ruby replied. "It's why I was so anxious to get home."

"You've been gone almost a month!"

"Well, I just found out a few days ago. That's when I became anxious."

"And before that?" Milo asked, eyebrows raised.

"I was, well, having fun. Learning," she looked over at the robots. "Milo, I was on an alien world with aliens. Robot aliens, but aliens! It was amazing!"

She looked over at her robot friends.

"Where did they come from?" Milo asked, "Who created them?"

"They don't know," Ruby said. She then went on to recount the situation about the robot's long-lost storage, their belief that it was contained within the junk DNA of some biological species, probably a species native to Earth.

She watched as Milo looked the robots over some more. He was now the second human to have met them. His life was likely to change somewhat, too.

She thought about how *her* life was going to change. Milo and her Uncle Blake had both tried to tell her she was famous. She wasn't sure what to do with that. Maybe all it would amount to would be a few interviews with the press, and then she could move on with her life. And still, she wasn't even sure what *that* meant. Less than a month ago, she was dead set on going to Titan, helping them to terraform Saturn's moon and set up a colony there.

Now, she wasn't sure. She thought maybe going back to

Earth for a while, possibly to finish earning her degree, wasn't such a bad idea. While she was there, she could figure out more about what happened to her mom when she was young. She realized now that the passage of time, combined with her young age when her mom died, probably contributed to an overall distortion of her early memories. She wanted to get them sorted out.

The console in front of her that was monitoring the atmosphere outside the mini-R-pod and in the hanger blinked green and made a soft chime.

"It's safe to open the hatch," Milo said.

Ruby heard the faint whir of processors spinning up in all three of the robots. They were just as nervous and anxious as she was.

Chapter 7

> Ruby <

From the moment Ruby stepped out of *Pecan Pi* and onto the hanger floor, she had one thought. *My uncles. Where are Uncle Blake and Uncle Logan?*

The other humans that made up the reception committee didn't seem concerned with what Ruby wanted and instead attempted to pursue their own agenda, which was to crowd her and get a look at the robots. The crowd of people included some she recognized and some she didn't. They were all chattering away and most of them were wearing the same shirt she saw moments ago: "I'm with robots!" The shirt also had an artistic reproduction of her face. In it, her hair was tied up, the same way it had been when she was on Location Zero. Was that taken from her message to her uncles?

She shook it off the second she saw them. Her uncles. Nothing could stop her from running to embrace them as soon as she was able. And she could see that nothing would have stopped them from pushing their way through the small mob to embrace her back.

While she was hugging the two of them at once, she recognized Robt Plampton's voice as he said to the crowd, "Give them a few moments, okay?"

After a few moments, which was not long enough, Uncle Blake broke the embrace but kept one hand on each of Ruby's upper arms. He looked into her eyes, raised his eyebrows as only he could, and asked, "Are you really okay?"

"Yeah, really. I am," Ruby responded, with a smile that she hoped conveyed that she was sincere in her claims of okay-ness and sorry that she had left and how much she had missed them and a dozen other emotions mixed in.

Uncle Logan was next, grabbing Ruby with a bear hug from behind. "Of course, she's okay! She's Ruby Palmer, galactic explorer!" He paused and looked into her eyes, making sure it was really her. His own glossed over. "Oh, Ruby! We thought…" he didn't finish that sentence. He didn't need to. Ruby knew what they thought, and she felt awful about it.

"Uncle Logan, Uncle Blake… I'm so sorry. I was being—"

"Selfish?" said Uncle Blake. Ruby nodded.

"Stubborn?" said Uncle Logan. Ruby nodded again.

"Surly?" said Uncle Logan.

"Okay, okay," Ruby said and spun out of Uncle Logan's embrace so she could face the two of them. "I truly am sorry. Worrying you two was the last thing I wanted to do. I just wanted—"

She stopped talking when she realized that it wasn't only her uncles who could hear her, but everyone in the crowd was silent and listening in.

"Can we go back to our quarters?" she asked, quieter than before. "I really want to shower in my shower."

"What about them?" Uncle Blake asked. He motioned to the robots that were positioned at *Pecan Pi's* hatch.

"Oh right! For a moment, I…" she didn't finish that thought and went over to the robots. "Guys, come on out." She gestured for them to leave *Pecan Pi.* They did, and as they did so, it was like there was an invisible force field emanating around them. The crowd moved so as not to come within ten feet of them.

"It's okay, everyone," Ruby said as she approached the robots and put a hand on SD's chassis. "They're friends. They're really nice. And funny."

Uncle Blake was the first to walk up to them. "Hi, my name

is Blake." He held out a hand in front of Disto.

"I haven't taught them about shaking hands, Uncle Blake. But that is Disto. That's short for Detailed Historian."

"Detailed? Historian?"

"Affirmative," said Disto.

"They know our language?" Uncle Blake directed that question to Ruby, softly so only she could hear.

"Yes, but here's the crazy part, Uncle Blake," Ruby whispered back. "They knew it, well, most of it, before I got there."

Ruby watched the color drain from Uncle Blake's face, and his eyes widened, but not quite with surprise. There was something else in his face that she couldn't read. She stored that away and would ask him later.

"This is Swell Driver. We call him SD. And that's Ambitious Technician. Also known as AT," Ruby finished out the introductions.

"That's an, uh, interesting nomenclature," said Robt Plampton, who had gradually sidled up to Uncle Blake's side. Uncle Logan had come forward, too, and was looking AT over.

"Oh definitely," said Ruby. "I'll have to tell you about the other robots I met."

"You'll be doing more than that," said Robt Plampton. "You'll get a chance to settle back in, but afterward, The Company has instructed me to put together a full debriefing. We are indeed going to hear about the robots, all the robots, and everything you experienced with these... aliens."

Ruby didn't know Robt Plampton very well. This might be only the second or third time she'd had reason to have a direct one-on-one interaction with him. But he was known as a pretty nice guy. Nonetheless, she wasn't thrilled with his tone. She looked to Uncle Blake for some comfort, but his face was stone. They'd obviously talked about this before she arrived.

"Sure, I guess," Ruby said. "Can we get quarters for the robots, too? I know that the one across the hall and down two units from ours was empty before I left."

"They're going to need to be debriefed as well."

Ruby looked at them and watched as they studied the brand new surroundings and the people staring back at them.

"I should be there. To help," she said. "Who is going to do it? The debriefing?"

Ruby watched as Robt Plampton pursed his lips. He clearly wasn't happy with what he was about to say.

"Professor Coronik. Prime Connector of the Church of the Blockchain. The Company has retained his services as an expert in AI and is sending him along with several of their own representatives."

Nothing was said for a few moments. Ruby couldn't understand why anyone from the Church would be involved. Looking around at the nearby crowd who were all listening in, she could see at the mention of the Church, a lot of faces wore an expression similar to Plampton's. This included her own uncles, who had always told her to stay away from that organization.

There was a small chapel on the station. Everywhere was required to have them, The Company couldn't even say no. She had peeked in once when she was young, out of curiosity. There were two people chanting something that she didn't understand. They seemed harmless enough.

"But sure—they can take the quarters in that hallway. It's still empty." Plampton nodded his head at Treszka Greene, Director of Station Ops—which was also known as Fundamental Operations and usually abbreviated to 'FUNOPS'—who was the person who typically handled these things and who shot darts from her eyes whenever anyone referred to her job as 'fun.' Treszka Greene tapped at her communicuff, which presented a holoscreen for her to continue to tap. Ready at a moment's notice to launch those eye darts, she nodded back at Plampton and then moved away from the group. Ruby hoped that meant she was making preparations.

"I'd like to walk them down there," Ruby said. "And then you can debrief me, I guess."

"After a short visit to the medical bay," Uncle Logan said.

"They're waiting to check you out, make sure you're as okay as you think." He winked that wink of his that Ruby had missed this past month. She smiled in return.

Chapter 8

> Ruby <

The robots were temporarily safe in quarters. Keeping them there was more for their protection than anything else. Ruby couldn't wait to show them around her home, and she figured their first tour should be a guided one and she should be the one to guide them.

All three robots agreed to stay put so she could go off and get a medical exam.

Now, in the medical bay, she was feeling… she didn't know how she was feeling. Uncle Blake and Uncle Logan were both there with her.

"You can let go, Uncle Blake," she motioned to his hand grasping hers.

"Nope," he responded. "You have no idea what we went through… thinking you were dead…" He looked at her and pushed a straggly piece of hair that had gotten out of her ponytail behind her ear.

"Don't lay too much guilt on her, she's been through a lot," said Uncle Logan.

Uncle Blake shot Logan a look that reeked of how much they'd been through, too. That look didn't make Ruby feel much better.

"I have to go get Sebastian from the Orville's," Uncle Logan said, then pecked Blake on the cheek, squeezed Ruby once more, and left.

"I'm so sorry, I really didn't mean to worry you. I really didn't," she looked at the floor.

"Well, you're back. And I just… I mean… I promised your mother…"

There was silence between the two of them for a few moments. Only the beeps emanating from a console behind them could be heard.

"About my mother…" Ruby said, but then was interrupted by Dr. Nora Lee, who walked in holding two tablets and what looked like a medical sweeper. Ruby observed she was wearing the same "I'm with robots!" shirt everyone else had, underneath her open lab coat.

Ruby leaned over to Uncle Blake, "Those shirts? Really?"

Blake chuckled. "I don't know who made them or is putting them out, but everyone seems to have one."

"Do you?"

Before Blake could answer, Dr. Nora Lee was standing in front of Ruby.

"Ruby Palmer!" she exclaimed. "Ahhh-mazing!"

"Thanks. I guess," Ruby said.

"No, really, you are the first person to leave the solar system! And I'm the first doctor to examine you. What you must have been exposed to. The radiation, different gravity fields! I can't wait to scan you. May I?"

Dr. Lee gestured to the examination table. Ruby hopped up and lay down. Dr. Lee put the tablets on a table next to the bed and then looked at the small console on the sweeper. She poked at it, presumably entering in whatever settings or directing it to look for who knows what.

Into her own communicuff, Dr. Lee said, "New diagnostic record. Patient's name, Ruby Palmer. Copy in last medical data as baseline."

Then she pointed the sweeper at Ruby's feet and continued to aim the sweeper at some place on Ruby's body, moving up and down and saying "hmm" to herself a lot.

After a few minutes, Dr. Lee put down the sweeper, picked

up a tablet, and started poking at that instead, with more mumblings. Words like "interesting" and "fascinating" emanated from her mouth, but as a mumble.

Then she said, "what the…?" and quickly reverted to medical sweeper again, aiming it at Ruby's abdomen.

Ruby looked over at Uncle Blake who could only shrug his shoulders.

"Everything okay, doctor?" he said.

"Yeah, but…" Dr. Lee was still involved in her devices.

"But…?" Uncle Blake and Ruby said in unison.

"Something is off. You haven't been gone from the station that long, but it's as if your digestive system, and your hormones are well… they're out of whack."

"'Out of whack?'" Ruby repeated. "Is that a professional term?" She saw the corner of Uncle Blake's mouth turn up.

"Yes, I took a course in diagnosing 'out of whack' in med school," Dr. Lee said, without missing a beat.

She moved a stool over to the side of the examination table. Like most furniture on Astroll 2, it had a slight magnetic connection to the floor, to ensure stability in the half-G environment. Dr. Lee sat on the stool, tablet in hand, and hooked her feet around a foothold to give her stability while sitting.

"Ruby, what have you been eating while you've been gone?" she asked very sternly.

"I uh, well, I mean, I ate the emergency rations that were on *Apple Pi*. But the robots had some stuff I could eat."

"What kind of stuff was it?"

"Well, most of it was mushy. The non-mushy stuff were like crackers. And it tasted like different things I recognized. Most of the time," she said recalling various memories of the variety of mushy and then eventually cracker-like meals she consumed.

Then she pushed herself to a sitting position with her arms. "Why? What's wrong with me?"

"It's malnutrition, for sure. But more than that. Your hormones are *out of whack*. And there's more heavy metals than there should be in a 19-year-old who's lived most of her life right here, eating primarily hydroponically grown food." Dr. Lee took a deep breath. "Let me put this another way. Some of your insides are that of a 47-year-old woman."

"But I don't feel 47," Ruby said.

"Are you sure? How tired have you been lately?"

Ruby thought about that. She'd slept pretty regularly. She didn't wake up feeling all that great, but she attributed that to the fact that she was sleeping on a very uncomfortable bed.

"Um, I guess I've been a little more tired than normal. But, I mean, the bed they had me on was not exactly luxurious…"

"Uh-huh," Dr. Lee said. "And how about the temperature. A little warm?"

Ruby thought about that. Yes, while on Location Zero, it felt like they had the temperature turned up, but then it went away. She assumed that the robots were consistently adjusting it to find the right temp for a human.

"Maybe?" Ruby said.

"Yup. Classic peri-menopausal symptoms. And not surprising given the state of your gut and hormones."

Dr. Lee hopped off the chair. "Not to worry. We have a simple treatment for this. You're going to spend time in my infra-red sauna and take some of these pills," Dr. Lee put some in Ruby's hand. "Twice a day for a week. That will reset your system while pulling out some of the toxins. The sauna will help get your system back into whack—also a technical term." She winked.

Ruby, as a 19-year-old, was aware of something called 'menopause' but, knowing it was something that she should have had three or more decades of life before she was even close to the right age for, had given it absolutely no thought. That was something older women dealt with, not her. In that moment, she realized she had no idea how old Dr. Lee was. Had she dealt with this herself? Was she talking to her as a doctor or a fellow sufferer? Did it matter?

Either way, she wasn't going to ignore Dr. Lee's diagnosis or prescription. And anyway, a bask in a sauna sounded pretty nice. As did getting a normal and refreshing good night's sleep in her own bed.

She took the pills sublingually, so they dissolved in her mouth. No water necessary.

"Perfect. I'll have the rest of the prescription assigned to you. It will be delivered to your quarters before your next dose, just as soon as they're printed."

Most medicines were formulated in a series of machines and printed into a form that could be dissolved right on the tongue.

"Can you imagine," Dr. Lee said, "that it wasn't all that long ago that this wasn't treatable. Women had to suffer, needlessly not knowing what was going on."

She had returned to her console and wasn't even looking at Ruby or Uncle Blake.

"Um, does that mean I can go?" Ruby asked. She looked at Uncle Blake who again, shrugged his shoulders.

"Oh, sure. You're fine," Dr. Lee said. "I want to continue to study your exam results. I'm surprised there isn't anything more wrong with you."

Ruby hopped down from the table.

"See, Uncle Blake? I told you I was fine."

"Sure. Old lady." He smiled. "That's going to be your new nickname."

"Did something happen while I was gone? When did you develop a sense of humor?"

"C'mon. Let's go back and see your robot friends. I might want to get a pre-briefing before your briefing," Uncle Blake said as he started to walk out of the medical bay. Ruby went to follow him, nearly bouncing past him.

"Wow," he said. "I don't remember you being that spry!"

"I guess it was the last month in Earth-like gravity," she said.

"Oh yeah," Dr. Lee called after, "her bone density is perfect. Better than perfect!"

"Interesting," said Uncle Blake. "You adjusted fine to their gravity?"

Ruby knew what he was getting at. For a long time, both of

her uncles had been on her to do her exercises regularly, in case she had to go back to Earth. Everyone on the station had to do it. Ruby had missed more sessions than she logged and did pay for it on her first week at Location Zero.

"Yeah, first couple days were rough, but obviously I got over it."

Uncle Blake smiled. "Good. And I can't wait to hear more about this Location Zero myself. Only 54 light years away, you said? That's remarkable!"

"How so?"

"Remarkable that we never detected anything so close to us before."

"I don't think they want to be detected," Ruby said. And then thinking out loud, "They have faster than light travel, sentient robots… so yeah, that makes sense that they'd have some kind of technology to prevent themselves from detection from the likes of us."

"Think they'd tell us about it?" Uncle Blake asked.

Ruby scrunched up her mouth. The whole reason SD brought her home in his ship was that they didn't want to send her off with an FTL drive. Well, that wasn't the whole reason. *Apple Pi* was still in pieces, sprawled out inside SD's ship.

"Unlikely," she finally replied. "But I don't think they'd be offended if you asked. Just don't get your hopes up."

"I never do," Uncle Blake said.

Chapter 9

> Uncle Blake <

A long, long time ago, on Earth, Blake Griffin had just returned to his apartment from a date. It was the best date he'd had in… well, maybe the best date he'd ever had. Logan Green was exciting and funny. He radiated a positive energy that Blake wished he had himself. Blake was doing his best not to get his hopes up. It happened every time after similar first dates. But this one felt different, and his hopes had settled on top of the largest roof in the city.

Their date consisted of meeting up at a coffee shop and then a spontaneous walk in the park since the UV levels were acceptable.

Back at his apartment, Blake's best friend, Jade Palmer, was on his couch, tapping at an ancient mobile computer she liked to use. Jade was almost always at his place. She didn't get along with her own roommates. Blake completely understood and offered to let her stay. He had the room. Jade insisted that it made sense for her to live someplace else, lest she prevent him from going on dates.

This date, in reality, was her doing. She had met Logan through a friend of hers at work, and once she found out that Logan was single, she knew instantly that Logan should meet Blake.

"How'd it go?" she said without looking up.

"It was," Blake sunk into the plush chair next to the couch, "in a word… it was wonderful."

Now Jade looked up. And smiled. "You're going to see him again?"

"We made plans for next Saturday. He knows a lake that's not too far away at some park that does kayak rentals. Apparently, there's a week or two left in the season before they close up till the spring."

"That's great!" Jade said. Her face was already back buried in her computer, but Blake knew that she meant it. They had been best friends since they were kids in Rhode Island. Now, they were young adults, living in Maryland—halfway between the re-re-named Washington D.C. and the City of Baltimore. Fresh from college, where they had both gone and studied nearly the same things and now worked similar jobs.

"Wait," Jade said and looked right at Blake. "Next Saturday? We have that meeting on Saturday."

"Right, in the morning. I haven't forgotten. The date doesn't start until lunchtime."

Jade relaxed. "You're not allowed to flake out on me, okay? I'm not going to this thing without you," she said. "Have you finished that bit of code I need?"

"I'm almost done."

What Jade was referring to was writing some code to hack some stuff. 'Some code' and 'some stuff' being the deliberately vague descriptions used by many hackers over the years.

They were both members of the Church of the Blockchain, but not really. They were both dreamers. They both had a love of outer space, the planets, and the thoughts of what was out there… and they were certain *something* had to be out there.

But the Church of the Blockchain—which started to distinguish itself somewhere around the year 2050—had managed to shut down practically all lines of research in that area. These days, no one was looking for alien life. But there were plenty of people looking for old computer data, and they were all willing to pay someone like Jade to find it.

So, the Church was paying her, on the books, to dig up data

on scores of servers they possessed.

But someone else was paying her too. A little less on the books, but it was currency that went into an account that, while it didn't have her legal name on it, she had full access to. She knew exactly who it was that was funding it—but not because they told her. It was a company funded by a company funded by a company, a couple times over, that was ultimately funded by the trillionaire known as Horus Zuliani. He had been in the news recently. Something about getting a team together to go to Titan. Given Ruby's—and Blake's interest—that wasn't money she was going to turn down.

But why the Church was interested…? On the surface, they seemed to simply be interested in data. And maybe they were. Jade hadn't found anything to the contrary.

However, there were several conspiracy theories permeating modern social networks. The one that Jade and Blake found most titillating was that the Blockchain already knew everything about Titan and was keeping it secret. The Blockchain wasn't a governmental entity, although it acted like one and practically controlled all the primary nation states on Earth. As such, they weren't accountable to anyone. Any evidence they might have in the search for extraterrestrial life would be locked up in their servers or their buildings, which some people called temples and other people called detention centers—due to how much time people spent in them.

Tucked away on the shore of Rhode Island as kids, Blake and Jade would daydream about aliens and about heading out into the solar system and exploring. As they got older, they learned about all the human colonies—the one on the Moon, the one on Mars, and the second one on Mars that failed—and the fact that no additional exploration out into and beyond the solar system was happening, the only exception being commercial asteroid mining activities. There were barely any telescopes that were looking outward, either. The ancient 'scopes, like the old James Webb Space Telescope and the Roman Space Telescope were now museum pieces and had been for decades. No one funded anything new.

There were too many problems on Earth. Instead, there was continued Earth-bound development into robotics and computing. In every generation there was a futurist who warned about the technological singularity coming, but every generation passed without it happening. But the amount of computers, robots, and computer power continued to increase. The Earth was hot and needed the ability to compute.

The Church was able to move computing resources—data centers—off Earth, which helped immensely. They heated up the Moon. In fact, the Moon colony was completely owned by the Church.

The Mars colony was operated by the world governments and was a research station. Not much was happening there.

The most interesting things happening in the solar system—at least to Jade and Blake— were out at Astroll 2. As well as Horus Zuliani, the Zubrinics Corporation, and their plans to get to Titan. As a completely commercial entity, while people might complain, there was no legal way to stop them.

Astroll 2 was the seat of a mining colony. The Company owned and operated it. Blake was set on going there someday and was actively trying to convince Jade that she should do the same.

Jade wasn't sure. There were a lot of computers and so much data to examine *here*. She was, in fact, a digital archaeologist. She was employed by the Church and spent her days hacking into old computers, organizing the useful data she found, and marking the non-useful data for deletion. In order to do this, she wrote many algorithms. She even won a prize.

The prize was this job with the Church. She was allowed to contract on the side, although her current contract wouldn't have been authorized if they knew about it.

Blake got a job with the Church, too, also in research, but of a different kind. At the time, when they were young kids just getting out of college, they believed the Church's promises that they could make a difference in helping their fellow man.

No sooner did they join they realized it was not about helping, but about controlling. And they realized that control extended to all forms of scientific research, including what they were most interested in: extraterrestrials.

This meeting that Jade referenced—it was a group of like-minded individuals. Members of the Church, but members who also had their eyes open to the truth. They were planning to expose the Church in the hopes that people would wake up, see the truth and then move on with their lives, free of the Church's control.

But that was next Saturday.

"What are you working on?" Blake asked. He was thinking about pulling out his own personal computer. He was coming down from his adrenaline high from his very successful date and was also thinking about watching a movie. "Anything interesting?"

"Huh? Oh… a game. Sort of."

"What do you mean, sort of?"

"It's a data archaeology hunt. One of those find all the incidences of 47…"

"Ah." Blake knew about those games. 47 was one of those numbers that people thought were deliberately hidden in vids and memes. It was a favorite of conspiracy theorists. Not that either he or Jade fell into that category.

Before he got too comfortable, he got up and went to the small kitchenette. "Lexy. Coffee, decaf," he said out loud. "Want anything?" he called back to Jade. She shook her head.

A device in the corner came to life and Blake heard the familiar gurgle of water being super-heated to brew a cup of coffee. He hoped that this time the decaf grounds wound up in the right spot. Last time, the automatic filler confused decaf for regular, and he was messed up for a week before he realized why.

After about thirty seconds, the drips came to a stop and a voice that was everywhere in the kitchen said, "Complete. Enjoy your beverage."

"Thanks, Lexy."

He of course knew that he didn't have to thank the computer but was in the habit of doing it anyway. In some way, he thought it made up for the times when he turned off all the active listening devices in the apartment so they could have truly private discussions. His landlord wouldn't be too happy that he was fooling around with the apartment computer systems, but only because the landlord was worried he would break something. There was no law against attempting to guarantee one's privacy.

Worst case, he wouldn't get his security deposit back.

Blake picked up the mug of coffee that was hopefully decaf and went back to the chair. "I'm going to put on a movie. Do you mind?" Again, Jade shook her head back and forth. "You staying right there all night? Again?" He smiled as he said this. He really didn't mind; he was just poking fun.

Jade nodded. "Yeah, just cover me with that blanket if I fall asleep."

"You should sleep," Blake said. "Maybe if you do, you'll look presentable and can go on a date yourself."

She shot him an 'are you kidding me?' kind of look. The look that friends can pass each other without hurting each other's feelings.

"Are you going to ever go out on one again?"

"I told you," she said. "I'm done with all that."

"Just because that jerk-boy-whose-name-we-don't-speak-of was a jerk doesn't mean you should swear off dating."

"Yeah, it kinda does. Look… when I'm ready… I'm going to do what my mom did."

"You know your mom is crazy?"

"She is. But I'm still here, right?"

Blake made a facial expression that indicated he couldn't argue with that.

"Exactly," Jade said. "All I have to do is go to the right cryo-center and boom. I'll have a kid. No jerk boys necessary. Besides, it would make it a family tradition. I think some of our ancestors did it as well."

Blake wished it was as easy for him. He knew he'd have kids one day, only it would be slightly harder. He had long thought, or wished, rather, that he would ask Jade to be a surrogate but wasn't sure she could do it—knowing she wanted kids, or at least a kid, of her own.

"Ok. New movie time. Comedy. Get ready to put your computer down and laugh with me."

Jade looked up and back at her computer and back at Blake. She closed the computer. "Fine. But I'm going to fall asleep as usual. Twenty minutes in."

"I know. I'll cover you with a blanket. And I won't wake you in the morning when I go out to run. Promise."

Chapter 10

> Ruby <

Ruby sat down with her tray of food. Milo and Inny were already there, at a seat by the windows, as far from the hallway and entrance as they could be, at Ruby's request.

While she was happy to have lunch with them, she already started to notice that when she was out in public, people were talking about her. Not *to* her but about her, as if she wouldn't notice. And at least half the people were wearing a shirt with her face on it. Maybe more than half since half were wearing the standard issue jacket that was typically worn on the station.

Milo and Inny had clearly been in the middle of some conversation which they promptly ceased having the second Ruby's tray touched the table.

"What were you talking about?" Ruby asked.

"Plampton," Milo said. "Word is, he's worried about all the people who are on their way here."

Ruby didn't need to ask why. She just looked down at her food, a little embarrassed at all the attention. Eh—who was she kidding. She was *a lot* embarrassed at all the attention.

It was all quickly forgotten as she looked at her food. Real food. Not mush. Real stuff. Although not fully what she what would have chosen for herself. At the moment, her meals were being selected by Dr. Lee as a part of her gut and hormone healing process. She wondered how long she could have stayed on the robot planet eating their various mushes before it became a problem.

At least now she knew that if or when—*was it if? Or was it when?*—she went back, she would need to pack her own food.

There was a special sourdough bread that was prepared for her. And a fruit bowl consisting of mango and coconut. She was certain that when she tasted it, she'd get the essence of ginger that she was currently smelling.

"Ooo! Mango!" Inny squealed. "That's probably the last for now until next First Mango Day. I want some!"

She took her fork and was about to steal a piece, but Ruby slapped her hand away.

"Hey! This is prescription food! Doctors' orders!"

Inny plopped back in her chair, feigning disappointment. Both Inny and Ruby knew this was not the first time Inny had tried to steal food off her plate, and nor would it be the last. They'd shared a meal together many times over the years.

But Milo—this was the first time she had sat down at a table in the mess with him. This also might have been the first time Ruby saw Milo and Inny interact in what felt like—forever.

"Now tell us everything!" Inny playfully demanded.

"Yeah," said Milo, "starting with how you lied to me in order to steal a mini-R-pod…"

Ruby hoped he wouldn't have put two and two together but how could he not?

"I'm sorry about that, Milo," Ruby said. She hoped the fact that she was indeed being sincere came across. "I was having a bad… a bad life. I don't know. It was stupid."

"You got that right," Milo said flatly.

"Do you hate me?" Ruby said with the smallest touch of flirtiness in her manner. She surprised herself that she could even do that. It felt almost manipulative or at the very least misplaced, but she hadn't intended it to be either.

"We thought you were dead…" Milo's voice went out a little at the last word. It was enough to silence the table.

Inny injected her version of cheer when she said, "Why are you being all depressing, Milo? You're making Ruby look like she's gonna vom."

"Vom?" Milo asked.

Inny raised an eyebrow as if Milo had asked her something incredibly stupid. "Vomit. Look, she's not dead! She's alive and she's going to tell us everything that happened. Right, Ruby?"

Ruby smiled. But then the smile went away as she saw Inny open up the note-taking app on her communicuff.

"Start with that guy you met for lunch before you left. Doctor... I can't remember his name!" Inny said.

"Inny..." Ruby started. "C'mon. I don't want you writing this down."

"*Someone* has to record this. Why not me? My first big journalistic break... interviewing the great Ruby Palmer! Now what was the name of that *yummy* man?"

The way Inny said 'yummy' made Ruby want to vomit, or vom, not from sickness, but from the overwhelming amount of attention paid to the details of her life. Maybe vomiting was the way to go. An educational experience for all the new people to Astroll 2 who've never seen what happens when someone loses their lunch in half-G.

> Milo <

She's having lunch with other guys. Okay, that does it. I have no chance other than as friends and coworkers.

These and 1000 other thoughts were rushing through Milo's mind, and he couldn't stop them. First, he thought she was dead. Then, he found out she was alive. Next, he was the second human to meet aliens all because of her. Now, he was having lunch with her—albeit with a chaperone.

But the icing on the cake—she was on a date with another guy.

"Inny! Sheesh! I can only imagine what you're thinking. So, stop it. It wasn't like that." Ruby asserted.

Milo perked up. *Ok, not a date!*

"That was Dr. Rush Guerrero. He's head of the Titan Expedition."

"Yeah, I've heard of him," Milo interjected, a little relieved to hear that she wasn't dating some good-looking guy—eh—man. But not so thrilled to hear she was interested in Titan. He searched his brain to remember the memes he had curated about Titan and could only remember the one that asked: if the oceans are all methane, is it covered in liquid farts? Not good conversation material. Instead, he focused on the meeting part. "What? Why? How were—no no… why were you meeting with him?"

"Because I want, or at least I wanted, to go to Titan," Ruby said. And the look she gave Milo said the rest. He got it. Now he understood what she was trying to do that day. She was going to take a mini-R-pod, that was set up for local run, all the way out to Titan.

"Holy spaceballs, Ruby," Milo said. "If I had known!"

"You never would have let me out of the hanger. Of course, I know that. That's why I didn't say anything."

Milo leaned back in his chair and looked at her. She was crazy. Well, not crazy, crazy, but she was some kind of crazy if she thought she could make it all the way to Titan from Astroll 2. He knew she never would have. How could she not see that? She was a good pilot, but the ships themselves were limited. Their comms were short range. Their fuel was—well, there was a lot of extra just in case of emergencies—but going to Titan was a far cry from an emergency—there was not enough. Ruby should have known that.

Oxygen and atmosphere should have been fine, but she could have easily lost power.

"I can't believe it, Ruby. That was…I don't even have the word for how gutsy dangerous that was."

He wanted to say other things to her. He wanted to tell her how he felt. He wanted to tell her that he wished it was just the two of them at this table, not three. Part of him wanted to show his admiration towards her bravery and accomplishments, and the other half wanted to scold her for worrying him sick. None of him wanted to admit how much he worried. Everyone did, sure, but Milo… He checked in with her little cousin and uncles as often as it felt appropriate. He wanted to tell her how he checked in with the asteroid monitoring team daily just in case *Apple Pi* would show up on their radar. He wanted to tell her how much he missed her sarcastic jabs when she was pretending that she didn't care about fitting in with the other pilots. He wanted to yell at her for ever leaving in the first place. He wanted to say a lot of things.

Nothing came out.

Instead, Inny picked up and left him thinking in the dust.

"Wow—I knew you weren't all that keen on going back to Earth, but Titan? It sounds *sooo* boring!"

"Based on where I've been the last month, yeah, it now seems that way," Ruby smiled. She was so cute when she smiled that Milo's anger at her deception was almost gone. One more smile like that, potentially directed in his direction, and he'd melt.

"Then what happened?" asked Milo.

"You guys know the rest. Swell Driver, SD… he found me out in space, used whatever beaming thing he had to disable my ship, and brought it onto his. Then we went back to what they call Location Zero. The rest is, as they say, robotic history!" Ruby said the last words as she took a mouthful of bread. Even talking with her mouth full, she was still cute.

Shake it off, Milo. She's not interested.

"And all these robots… they're different," Inny continued. Milo could tell she was struggling with finding the right words and concepts.

Ruby continued. "Oh, yes! *So* different. They're sentient. I have no idea how that happened or is even possible. They don't either, although I don't think they understand the concept of sentience versus non-sentience. They've um… met others…"

Milo sensed something there. "Excuse me?" he chimed back in.

"Forget I said anything. I shouldn't get into that..."

"No, no… you're going to have to repeat yourself," Inny looked at Milo, and they both nodded in agreement.

Ruby pursed her lips, swallowed what was in her mouth and

leaned over the table and encouraged Milo and Inny to do the same.

In a much lower voice, Ruby continued. "They've met other species. I was told not to talk about it. 'Cause it would freak people out."

They all leaned back once again in their respective chairs. Ruby continued to eat. Milo didn't know what to do or say. Not that that was unusual for him.

"You're not going to write that down?" Ruby said to Inny.

Milo looked at Inny, who was in the process of digesting the same information and wasn't paying attention to her communicuff. He had never seen anyone's eyes look wider.

"I'll admit it. I'm freaked out!" Inny said, not blinking for so long that her eyes glossed over.

"See?" Ruby said.

Milo put a fork in his food, and for a moment, allowed himself to think that there was someone else putting a fork in their food somewhere else in the galaxy, possibly thinking the same thoughts he was thinking right now. Possibly making the same discovery at the same moment—that there were other alien beings in the universe. Maybe they didn't know who or where, but just knowing that they existed.

He had so many questions. He wondered for a moment if humans were the last to the party. He wouldn't be surprised. He was often the last to any party. Parties made Milo very uncomfortable.

"Look," Ruby said, breaking the uncomfortable silence. "I can't believe I'm saying this, but they're really nice. SD and the others. You should spend some time with them. They're funny, too. Especially when they tell me that they understand what I'm saying, but then mess it all up."

"Robot. Aliens," Inny said.

Milo had already spent a little time with them when he brought them back from the large ship that was holding a parking position relative to the station. They talked about finding a different parking orbit for a few reasons, not the least of which is that it was currently right in the middle of the approach path for incoming ships, and they had to keep that path clear or incoming ships would have to compute less efficient trajectories.

Milo and SD would be making a special trip later that evening to re-park SD's ship. So, spending more time with at least one of the robots was already in the cards.

They had tried asking ships to maneuver around, and one did—the one that was carrying a VIP and some press. It burned too much fuel. At this point, it was easier to ask the robots to move their ship. The robots agreed and now that activity was on the schedule for later that day. Which reminded Milo that he wanted to ask:

"Are you coming with me and SD later? To move his ship?"

Ruby's brow furrowed. "No," she said. Clearly, she wasn't happy about it.

"Will you at least stay in the control center in communication?"

And Ruby's brow instantly returned to its natural state, and she brightened. "Of course! Happy to!"

Milo thought it was sweet how transparent Ruby could be about her emotions sometimes and how concealed she could be other times.

Again, she continued to shovel food in her mouth. She really wasn't a neat eater. He'd get over that if he ever had another chance to eat with her. Maybe next time without this chaperone who chimed in again.

"Okay, so… robots! Tell us!"

"Like I said, you should meet them. Spend time with them yourself. I'll introduce you. I need to finish eating first. This food is *soooo* good."

They all smirked at that. Station food, particularly station mess food, while not the worst in the solar system, wasn't known as being the best either. Although Milo couldn't tell you why. Most of it was fresh, as it was grown in the hydroponics bay right on the station.

They let Ruby finish every bit that was on her plate.

After a few minutes, Milo had an odd feeling. He looked

around. Every table in the mess was full. That wasn't normal. People were talking at every table, and occasionally pointing, and definitely looking—at Ruby.

He knew several of the people. Heck, one of his team members was there with his station girlfriend—separate from the girlfriend he talked about who was still on Earth. Many of the people he recognized as other station residents, even though he wasn't personally acquainted with them. And several he didn't recognize at all. They must be the people who came on that recent ship or the one that preceded Ruby's arrival.

One of these was holding up a communicuff, clearly trying to take a picture. Milo stood up and put himself in between Ruby, who was mid-chew, and the voyeur.

"Hey! What are you doing?" he called out, surprising himself that he was standing up and yelling at a stranger.

"Taking pictures of Ruby Palmer, what does it look like?"

"She's eating. Can't you see that? Come back later."

"She's eating, and she's famous. People want to see famous people doing normal things."

"But Ruby might not want her picture taken."

"Irrelevant."

Milo knew there was nothing else he could say. He turned to Ruby. "You okay? You guys want to leave?"

Ruby looked around Milo at the room of people. Her eyes opened wide as she, too, caught sight of the unusual quantity of people in the mess. She swallowed and said, "yeah. I'm done."

She stood up, and half the mess stood up, too.

She sat back down, and so did they.

"Um, this is weird," she said. Milo took her tray to the reco-recycler and then came back. He gestured that she should get up. She did, as did Inny.

"Let's just go," he said.

Half the room stood up, too. They didn't stop Ruby from exiting the mess, but they certainly followed her out. Now it was obvious that multiple people were taking her picture.

"Where to?" Milo asked.

"I want to go meet the robots," Inny said.

"Wait, didn't you just say you were freaked out?" Ruby asked.

"Uh, yeah, but freaked out in a *good* way!" Inny beamed. "Maybe I can get them to give me some quotes I can use." Inny trailed off lost in thought.

"I wonder what they'll think of TERP." Milo said. He genuinely was curious about another take on the AI that seemed to be in the news and everywhere.

"What's TERP?" Ruby asked.

"Oh wow, you've been back a whole day, and you haven't heard? Come on, we'll fill you in," said Milo.

Chapter 11

> Professor Coronik <

Professor Lloyd Coronik unbuckled his seat belt and floated towards the front of the passenger cabin to get himself a soda. Unfortunately, the selection on these passenger transports was limited to the generic brand flavors of orange, brown, and yellow. He eyed the three and tried not to let the pedestrian accommodations chip away at his psyche.

One might think that Professor Coronik would have taken one of the fancier ships, one that was larger and could spin to produce gravity, or—even more preferable—one with a better selection of food and beverages, but this was all that was available on such short notice.

One might also come to this conclusion because of Professor Coronik's notable position in the Church of the Blockchain. He was a Prime Connector. One of only three in the whole Church—the wealthiest church to ever exist. It would be logical to guess that such an organization would own its own ship. Or its own fleet.

Except that church officials rarely left Earth and generally were opposed to doing so.

Professor Coronik, however, determined, along with his fellow Prime Connectors, Charlotte Henry and Yesenia Aziz, that there was a worthwhile reason to leave the planet: to meet Ruby Palmer, the first human to do so many things. And her robot companions. He couldn't imagine the technology they possessed—imagination was not one of his strengths. Professor Coronik's job was to ensure that any technology transfer that was likely going to occur, would do so with the Church as the initial recipient. The only way to do that was to establish a relationship with the robots before they came to Earth and established their own relationship with one of the increasingly useless world governments.

Professor Coronik, drink packet in hand, used his other hand to propel himself back along the aisle and into his seat.

To make things worse, this ship was completely full of people. And to make it even worse, the entire trip would take five days.

Not that this was slow. What these types of ships lacked in comfort, they made up for in speed. That was the other reason he didn't try to buy someone's seat on a more luxurious ship. The luxury ships were slower and slow was not his preferred method of travel. Especially not on a time-sensitive mission as this.

His seat wasn't quite a seat. It was a little more like an angled bunk. One could stretch out and sleep but needed to stay strapped in at quite a cumbersome angle to avoid floating away.

And it was one person per side of the cabin.

As Professor Coronik was strapping himself back in, he caught the eye of the individual in the seat across the aisle from him. He had preferred not to get involved in any conversation with strangers along the way and had managed to avoid eye contact. He traveled alone, and kept his privacy settings set to max, as anyone with glasses would see.

Despite his efforts, this time he made eye contact with someone who might have been about his age and was clearly not wearing percepto-glasses. It was hard to tell with the obvious makeup and non-glass enhancements they wore. Not that it mattered. Coronik still did not want to engage in conversation.

"Hey, I know you," this individual, who had been awkwardly strapped in on their side, reading a tablet, propped themselves up on an elbow and looked Professor Coronik up and down. "I write about you all the time."

"Oh?" Coronik said, trying not to sound too interested, already making the assumption that this person was press. Unwanted press.

"Yes, I've written about the Blockchain in nearly every research paper I've published."

So, not press, Coronik thought to himself. He must have accidentally made some movement or gesture that signaled this person to continue because they did.

"Yeah, I'm a doctoral student of philosophy at large from the University of the Gakkel Ridge. I specialize in the Church, and technology, and the history of all that. I would *love* to talk to you about it. I'm working on a paper right now that compares TERP to—"

Coronik studied this individual before responding. He couldn't tell if this was an eager fan or someone who thought that he'd be genuinely interested in what they had to say. Not that he hoped it was the former, but he was certainly not the latter.

"Maybe once we get to the station. I'd like to sleep right now," Coronik thought that was the only way to get out of an unwanted conversation before it continued. He had no interest in being interviewed as 'research' for anyone's paper, academic or news. Once on Astroll 2, he was certain he'd be able to keep this individual out of his way. He was on a mission and had no time or patience for such distractions.

"Sure, sure. I was getting myself ready to sleep, too. Just some light reading. History. Do you ever read any history? Fascinating stuff what they didn't know only a couple hundred years ago."

"Mmm," Coronik said, attempting not to encourage a second wave of banter.

"My name is Link Vala, by the way. Or 'B-T-W' as they used to say in the early days of networking and the internet. That's what I'm studying right now. There was a lot of ridiculous things they said and did back then. I wish I could have known someone from that time. Do you know there were some really long-lived people? Their stories were recorded, but I would have just loved to talk to them. Face to face, ya' know? Today's centenarians are their grandkids, so it's not the same."

"Really, I'd like to get some sleep," Professor Coronik said. And begrudgingly, because now he figured it was the only way he would achieve silence, "maybe we can talk later."

"Sure, sure. 'Nite." And Link Vala turned their tablet back on, and Professor Coronik turned off the illuminating lights in his compartment.

Link Vala spoke up in an obnoxiously loud whisper, "Is it okay if I have my tablet light on?"

The light didn't bother Professor Coronik, only noise, so he grunted a curt, "Sure," and hoped that would be the last thing he heard for a while.

"Are you sure, you're sure?" Link Vala continued and Coronik wished he knew what it would take to convince them. "I can turn it of it you're—"

"It's really fine."

There was a blissful moment of silence where Coronik was able to achieve some measure of coziness in the seat that was clearly not designed for cozy. He was just on the edge of a hypnagogic dream, when he heard, blaring from across the aisle, "… and *Palmer* is the one with access to advanced *robots*…"

"Sorry, sorry!" said Link Vala, clearly flustered. "My pur-fi connection just went wonky."

Professor Coronik didn't feel the need to provide any acknowledgment of this. He kept his eyes shut and tried to pass the time by sleeping, with limited amount of success.

Chapter 12

> Detailed Historian <

Disto occupied space in a room with SD and AT. The room was called 'living quarters' and the three of them were instructed to occupy this space until Ruby returned for them.

"There is not a lot of space to move around," AT complained.

Complained or uttered a statement of fact? The humans put a lot of objects in their rooms. Objects that were known as furniture. Disto and the others understood the concept and were wondering if it made sense to ask if some of these objects could be removed.

They decided against it lest their human hosts think they were unappreciative of their hospitality. Especially since Disto still needed information from them.

"I am going to try and link to their computer console," Disto said after a thorough survey of the room. Before Ruby left them, she attempted to show the three robots where a device she called a keyboard materialized in the air.

"I don't see anything," Disto had said. AT and SD nodded in agreement.

Ruby had looked as if she was poking her fingers in the air, and then all of the sudden something materialized under her fingers as she poked away.

"There. I made the keyboard green. The default color is red, something I know you don't normally see. And ugh—there's probably going to be other things you don't see because of that. We use red a lot—I'm not going to be able to change colors on everything."

"I'm sure we'll get by."

Disto was looking at the keyboard and recognized the individual components that made up Ruby's native language.

"In some ways," Ruby said, "when you start looking at the system, you'll see that it's not too different from your own. There's a main menu that you can always come back to by pressing this key here."

Disto nodded that he understood.

"Need anything else? I promise I won't be gone long."

They said no, and she left.

SD had been very quiet since arriving. Disto didn't want to disturb his thoughts. He browsed through the system until he found what he remembered Ruby calling "ancient vids." She had explained that this was entertainment—made-up stories, not historical records. He marked these to come back to later and watch. Rather than choose one or two, he was going to watch all of them. Maybe SD would be interested as well.

AT, on the other hand, had been just as curious as Disto was about everything and anything, often pointing at objects and wondering how they worked. Several times he remarked out loud, "I wonder if they would let me take it apart."

After making the same remark multiple times, AT settled himself by connecting into the wall that allowed him to manipulate the wall itself. It was odd, but at least he was quiet and occupied.

But now, what was on Disto's circuits was finding more samples of non-human life that he could test.

He accessed the computer via the hovering keyboard and pressed the main menu button.

And nothing there made any sense.

Luckily, that's when Ruby returned. She stood in the doorway, and Disto could see her Uncle Blake standing behind her. He touched her arm. Disto watched the two of them exchange some form on non-verbal communication. They both distorted their faces and then Blake was leaving them. Ruby had tried to describe the title 'uncle,' but Disto's circuits had a hard time processing any of the relationships that Ruby described as familial. 'Familial' itself was a concept he couldn't claim to grasp in its entirety. Connections between humans who made other humans. Disto was made from a template, by a Hall, and couldn't imagine he would have any type of fondness for the Hall the way Ruby did with her uncles. Objectively, it made sense, but the sentiment... not so much. Nevertheless, he at least understood there was a connection between Ruby and Blake that was closer than Ruby and most of the other billions of humans and Disto hoped to talk to him at some point.

"Ready for that tour of Astroll 2 I promised?" Ruby said.

"Yes, indeed!"

Two of the three robots lined up and Ruby led them out into the hallway. The third, AT, was still sitting by the wall, plugged in, and it now occurred to Disto that AT had produced no sounds in a while.

"AT?" Ruby said, "Are you... feeling well? Is that the right thing to ask?"

AT moved its soft face-screen that was on its top, soft chassis to face her. To Disto, it looked like it was taking more effort than it should have.

"I don't..." AT trailed off. He looked less inflated than normal.

Ruby rushed over and knelt by his side, followed by Disto who said, "There is a built-in diagnostic we should run."

"Okay, how do we do that?" Ruby asked.

"I have..." the amount of effort it took AT to produce audible vocalizations was palpable and produced an unpleasant sensation in Disto's circuits. "Have... have... run diagnostic."

"And?" Ruby asked. Disto analyzed the tone of her voice and determined what he detected was a mix of urgency and fear.

"Virus," he responded. "Activated accidentally..."

Ruby responded by immediately disconnecting AT from the wall. The action startled Disto, but AT looked a tiny bit better.

"Thank..." he said.

"Are you functioning properly now?" Disto asked. "It is unfortunate that you didn't say anything before now. We could have helped sooner."

"The device," AT said, indicating the wall, "it was trying to suppress my virus."

Ruby flipped down a small panel on the side of the wall AT had been connected to and made another keyboard appear in front of her. Disto watched her fingers glide around, and she didn't quite frown but scrunched her lips together.

"This is a touchscreen wall. It's another version of a computer that is connected to our system. Like all devices, it has virus protection, malware scanning, and even parental controls. See?" She took one of her digits and pressed it to the wall. Disto recognized the letter 'f' that appeared, but nothing else happened after. "I guess the good news is that AT's virus didn't get into our systems. The computer did its job."

"Ah!" SD made a squeak. He, too, had been a container of silence but SD came alive at this. "If there is good news, then there is bad! Good and bad are opposites that go together." His coloring indicated a sense of pride in understanding Ruby. Disto liked that SD's behavior was representative of his normal self.

"Is there indeed bad news, Ruby?" Disto asked.

"Uh yeah," she said and waved her hand at AT. "AT has a virus. Look at him."

They all looked.

"Suggest... deactivate... until... return to Location Ze..." AT sputtered.

"Deactivate?" Ruby exclaimed. "What does that mean? How...?"

Before anyone could answer, AT had his soft appendage touching the side of his face-screen. After a moment, and before anyone could not only answer but protest or object or ask more questions, AT was deflating. Along with that, his face-screen went dark, clearly receiving no more power. As he deflated, the soft material that comprised his surface shrank together as well, the smoothness turning wrinkly and collapsing inward. After a handful of tics, AT was reduced to something Ruby could pick up and hold in the palm of her hand.

Which is what Disto saw her do. She held AT in her two cupped hands and looked over at Disto.

"What just happened?" she said.

"He deactivated himself."

"Yeah but… what… I don't…"

"I suggest you hold on to him. Perhaps in one of your clothing compartments. When we return to Location Zero, we will reactivate him."

"Ok," Ruby said. "But can you… also…"

"If you are asking if I can also deactivate and 'shrink' I think is the word, then yes and no. Yes, I can be deactivated as can anything. That second capability is unique to robots of AT's type. If I, or if SD here, were to be deactivated, we would not be as," Disto wanted to choose the right word, "portable."

Disto watched Ruby watch AT and after a few tics, she did indeed place AT in an inner pocket of the article of clothing she called a 'jacket.'

"Are we going on our tour now?" SD asked.

Disto watched Ruby blink. Bios, at least humans, had unique ways of processing data. Ruby, in particular, would oscillate the covering over her optical sensors. Disto admitted that he didn't quite understand the link between those actions, but he was a Historian, not a Zookeeper.

Eventually, Ruby said, "I've arranged to use the lift, since you guys aren't suited for most of the ladders that we use to get in between the rings. The lift is usually used for moving equipment around."

"Are we equipment?" Disto asked.

"No," Ruby said, and Disto found himself grateful that there was no pause to consider a response. "However, you lack certain, um, physical features that make ladders convenient."

"We don't have lower appendages like you."

"Legs. Exactly," she said. "But where we're going, you don't need legs."

Chapter 13

> Professor Coronik <

"Prepare for docking," came a voice over the speaker system. "Ensure that everything in your seat has been stowed. Ensure that you are buckled in the five-point-five restraining system. The Company welcomes you to Astroll 2 and we hope you've enjoyed the ride."

Professor Coronik had nothing to stow so he relaxed once more and closed his eyes. He had been buckled in for a while and had spent most of the journey sleeping. The lack of prolonged physical activity left him dazed and drowsy.

His unintentional traveling companion, Link Vala, shuffled around quite a bit to put everything back in its place and was very busy futzing with the restraint system. When they were done, they said, "OK, once we dock, what's the plan?"

"Excuse me?"

"We're both here to see the robots. What's our plan? Our approach?"

"I'm here to debrief the robots on behalf of the Church. There is no 'we' or 'our' in my activities."

"Oh c'mon. There's so much to figure out here and the two of us approaching them would—Well, I'm sure it would be more than two? Me and your team."

"No, on this trip, it's just me. There will be a team back on Earth."

"On Earth? They're going back to Earth?"

"Of course. We have the best laboratories and facilities there… for examination. Not to mention some of the best roboticists. Astroll 2 doesn't have the facilities to handle something of this magnitude."

"But these are aliens. They're not just robots. They're alien robots…"

"I'm well aware."

With that, a tone erupted in the background that signaled that they were in the hanger of Astroll 2. A red light was illuminated at the front of the cabin signaling that they were not yet ready to disembark.

"A few moments and we'll have you all disembarking to Astroll 2," the friendly voice came over the speaker system again. "The docking hanger needs to be repressurized. This is standard procedure for those of you on your first trip here."

Professor Coronik only raised a small eyebrow at this. He was well aware of standard procedures since they were the same for all space travel and while this was indeed his first time on Astroll 2, this was hardly his first time in space.

"Where are you staying?" Link Vala interrupted his thoughts.

Luckily, before he could decide how to respond, the disembark light turned green, signaling that they could get off the vessel.

Professor Coronik managed a faint smile that exuded an air of no-time-for-small-talk, grabbed his one bag—he had luggage that would be delivered to his room for him—and politely, but with purpose, weaved around the other people who were still gathering their things.

Once on the deck of Astroll 2, he felt…woozy. No, that was the low gravity. It was higher than the vessel that brought him here but lower than Earth. He knew to expect that. The air also smelled like overly recycled air, with a tinge of cinnamon. Or was that cardamom. Something smelled sweet in a homey kind of way. He looked around… maybe that was a smell from one of the disembarking passengers.

He continued looking around. Lots of faces he didn't recognize, and then… there was the person who was his designated contact, Myra Kaling, Deputy Director of Astroll 2.

"Professor Coronik, welcome," she held out a hand.

"Nice to meet you in person," Professor Coronik said. "Thank you for arranging this."

"Of course. Let's get you through on-boarding, and then I'll escort you to your quarters."

Professor Coronik nodded and let Myra lead the way.

She brought him to a console operated by a person who asked to see his documentation.

"You have a human doing the job of an AI," he said to Myra as he pressed a button on his communicuff and poked at the image that appeared until it produced his identification. He turned the image so that the superfluous person could scan it.

"Professor Lloyd Coronik. Arrival time logged. Departing… Hmm… we don't have a departure date for you."

Myra assured the documentation processor that all was in order. As she was turned away from him, Coronik eyed a very small tattoo just below and behind her earlobe. It was the mark of the Church of the Blockchain. Coronik smiled. Believers were everywhere.

While another few moments passed, Coronik saw Link Vala talking with another processor. He could see from his vantage point their forearm. It was held at an angle that the hologram image above it could be seen by the processor they were talking to as well as himself. It was an image of Ruby Palmer. Coronik started to wonder if he should have found out a little more about who Link Vala was and what they were really doing here. Hopefully, someone was responsible for Ruby Palmer's calendar and meetings and would certainly ensure that someone of his stature met with her and her robots before any of the riff-raff.

"I will say," Myra interrupted his thoughts and gestured that they make their way away from processing, "that as nice as it is to have you here, Prime Connector, I'll be happy when you leave. I presume those robots, those aliens, will be leaving with you."

"Well, yes, yes, of course," he responded, although he wasn't focused on her words, but was following her in an uncoordinated motion down the ring, presumably to where his quarters would be for the next few days. He was trying to get his bearings in this unfamiliar place, lest he come off as a fumbling buffoon.

"Sir?" Myra said, stopping at the foot of a ladder. Coronik realized she had been talking the whole time.

"TERP will have something to say about this, I presume?" Myra said, presumably repeating herself.

"Well, yes, TERP gets a say in everything. We designed it that way. Of course." Coronik hoped his response was the right one. Reading Myra's face, which relaxed somewhat, told him it was. Coronik then followed her up—or was it down—the ladder and down the much narrower hallway of another station ring.

She stopped after a few bouncy steps, smiled and gestured to the door that was now in front of them. "Do you want to rest or...?"

"I'll just drop my bag down. I want to meet your... guests... as soon as possible."

Chapter 14

> Detailed Historian <

"On behalf of the Church of the Blockchain, I welcome you."

"We have already been welcomed by several individuals," Disto said. He understood that Bios had their rituals, but this one seemed repetitive and redundant. Quite unnecessary, he thought.

Disto and SD were lined up on one side of a table in what Ruby had called "Robt Plampton's leadership conference room." Disto had wanted to ask why a specific room was needed for discussions, but Ruby looked like she was tired. She was here, too, as was her Uncle Blake, both of whom occupied the same side of the large table.

Robt Plampton was at one side that was perpendicular. Facing the robots, from the opposite side of the table was Myra Kaling. Next to her was the human who had just offered yet another welcome, Coronik.

All the humans were standing, but Coronik was the only one attempting to keep himself stable by placing the tips of his digits on the table. It wasn't working very well, and he continued to have a certain back and forth motion that made him look uncomfortable. Disto wondered why no one offered to provide him a stabilizing device.

"Well, I welcome you as well. I hope we can establish open relations with your… people." Coronik stumbled over that last word, and nearly pushed himself away from the table as he lifted one of his hands. "With your kind, I mean." He simultaneously cleared his throat and reached back for the edge of the table. "Are you authorized to speak on behalf of your government?"

Uncle Blake chimed in, "Professor Coronik, I thought this was going to be a simple introduction, not an overture to diplomatic relations."

Every movement Coronik made appeared to be in slow motion. He gripped the table harder, Disto could see the muscles on top of his hands and starting up his arm contract. Then he blinked and while blinking, angled himself so he was facing Uncle Blake.

"Ruby here has summarized all the debriefing points very nicely," Coronik said, and just when Disto was certain Coronik was doing everything he could to not let go of the table, he unclenched the ends of his appendages from that table and faced Ruby's Uncle Blake, "May I speak with you over here?"

Uncle Blake joined Coronik in a corner of the room that was the furthest point from where he and SD had been placed. That wasn't very far in this modest room, maybe five appendage lengths away.

Even though they lowered the volume of their emanations, Disto could still hear what the humans were saying. Not that he was attempting to listen in, it was just that they weren't as quiet as they thought.

As such, he heard Coronik tell Ruby's Uncle Blake that caution was indicated, and that they had to treat this diplomatically, lest a whole army of robots come and invade this solar system.

Before he could fully process the meaning of the word 'army' in this context, he heard Uncle Blake defend the robots saying that if that was what they wanted to do, it would have already been done. They obviously had the means.

"Obviously. And now we need to make sure we have the means," Coronik said.

"Who do you mean by 'we'?"

When Coronik didn't answer that, Uncle Blake crossed his arms and said, "That's what I thought."

Then they were back at the conference table, Uncle Blake spoke directly to the robots, "Guys, don't answer any questions that make you... uncomfortable. If you're able to become uncomfortable that is."

"Oh, we are indeed!" SD responded enthusiastically. "'Uncomfortable' is one of the signs that a robot needs a repair. Coronik, we—"

"It's Professor Coronik," said Professor Coronik as he tugged on his suit. "I have multiple degrees. Four, to be precise."

"Then shouldn't we call you Professor Professor Professor Professor Coronik?" Disto asked.

Professor Coronik's jaw tightened. "One 'professor' is sufficient. And which robot are you? Which one is the technician?" He was looking at SD.

Disto chimed in, "I am Detailed Historian. My companion is Swell Driver. Ambitious Technician is currently incapacitated until he can access maintenance."

The human, Coronik, Professor Coronik, was using his optical sensor to scan both of them. "I see," he finally said. "And who programmed you?"

"The Hall of Templates," Disto responded confidently. "Same as any and every robot."

"And who is in charge of the Hall of Templates?" Professor Coronik asked.

"The Core, of course," Disto continued to be engaged.

"And who is in charge of this Core?"

Disto responded, "The Core leadership is formed by representatives from all the Halls and Agencies."

"Well, that is quite fascinating," said Professor Coronik flatly. "Quite fascinating, well...indeed. Who set up this structure? Start at the beginning."

"We don't know. I assume when you, what was the word," Disto paused to look it up, "oh yes, when you 'debriefed' Ruby she explained our current situation with our historical records."

At the mention of her name, all optical sensors—human and robot—went to Ruby. She didn't add anything, but her own optical sensors dilated when she perceived everyone looking at her.

"Let's move on to something else that has been bothering me about your story," Professor Coronik said. "Ruby's mini-R-pod, *Apple Pi.* You disassembled it?"

"That was a mistake," Disto responded.

"Well, what a mistake. That was not your property, and that's a known way to learn the ins and outs of someone else's technology. Can we learn about your technology the same way?"

Disto didn't like what he thought this Bio might be implying. "No, you may not take SD's ship apart. Unlike Ruby, who obviously had a way to be brought home, we do not."

"But you will tell us about your faster-than-light technology, of course."

"I must have the words 'of course' mistranslated. Because no, we cannot do that. We are not authorized to make that kind of technology transfer."

Disto didn't feel as if he needed a repair, but he felt something unpleasant. He was starting to wonder if there were multiple meanings to the word uncomfortable. If there were, then this was it.

> Professor Coronik <

Professor Coronik, Lloyd, knew when not to push. Even if it wasn't the thing he was trying to get. He was not interested in faster-than-light technology, usually just abbreviated as 'FTL,' although he knew many others who were, and that they'd pay practically anything to get it, including every world government that still existed. If he could get *his* hands on FTL first, he would gladly accept it and reap all the associated benefits.

But that wasn't his primary interest. Instead, he wanted to take apart the robots. He wanted to see how they tick. He wanted to know what made them sentient. The Church had been working on AI for a long time. Claims of sentient AI came and went, each one getting disproved. The latest AI experiment, TERP, the one he had personally convinced the President of North America to adopt to run the government was, well, behaving unpredictably. Not that anyone knew. But everyone had convinced Coronik that blockchain tech was suitable for AI purposes and he sanctioned the project, pouring resources upon resources into it.

"Well, I certainly understand that." Lloyd said. "We have similar laws and limits on technology transfer between various nation-states on Earth that go back hundreds of years. In fact, I'm authorized to invite you there…"

The robot that called itself Disto perked up.

"Yes, please," it said. "We need to go to Earth. To test samples."

"Oh yes, I read that in the debriefing report, too." Coronik responded. "Well, there will be a few challenges, but I'll help. With the Church of the Blockchain behind you, there should be no problems."

"What kind of challenges?" Ruby asked.

"Well, Ruby, a lot of people are not thrilled with the discovery of alien intelligence out there, especially because it is different to us. There is a growing movement to have the robots banned from Earth before they even get there!"

"What? Are you kidding me? These are the nicest…"

"The nicest kidnappers?" Coronik asked.

"Yeah, I get what it looks like. But they didn't harm me, and I'm back in one piece. Everything is fine."

"Well, either way, they clearly do not operate on the same moral level as us which alone is concerning. A lot of people see this as the start of an invasion."

"I'll say it again," Uncle Blake added, "that if they wanted to invade, they would have. A long time ago."

"We are not invaders," Disto said. "We simply want to find our data."

"Well, you are referring to data that you might have

embedded in one of the species on our world. That is also something a lot of people have an issue with. Many do not like the concept of genetic manipulation—for any reason. To think that you've changed our animal population—"

"It's just in the junk DNA," Ruby interrupted. "It wouldn't change a thing."

"Well, 'junk DNA' and 'genetic manipulation," Coronik stood up straight and was pleased with himself for being able to continue to use the most technical words in the conversation, "are complex concepts that are hard to describe to the average person." He swallowed, knowing that he wasn't sure he knew what it meant and would get the computer to explain it to him later. After all, he wasn't the average person but the Prime Connector with a series of degrees.

Ruby crossed her arms. "I learned about genetics in school when I was twelve."

"Nonetheless," Coronik said, "TERP is going to want to have a say in this matter."

"TERP? Why would your budget-crunching AI have anything to do with this?" Ruby shook her head.

Coronik opened his mouth while he tried to formulate a response, but Ruby continued, "I hate that I'm suggesting this but maybe we should do a news broadcast? If people were to see SD and Disto, and see how harmless they are…?"

"Well, you're going to get your chance at that," Coronik said. "Sooner than you think…"

Chapter 15

> Blake <

"Blake, you need to see this!" Jade said as she burst into Blake and Logan's apartment, baby wrapped around the front of her body in the carrier that they'd gifted her.

They were supposed to meet up later in the day, take Jade's baby, Ruby, for a walk, and talk about the Church and their plans. Apparently, Jade didn't want to wait until later.

Blake stuck his head into the hallway before closing the front door. Out of habit, he looked both ways to see if anyone was around or annoyed at the early morning noise. There was no one. The last thing he saw before shutting the door was one of a series of framed posters mounted on the other side of the hallway that promoted the commandments of the Church. The one located directly outside his apartment read, "Thou shalt not delete data."

People didn't need to be told that, however. The amount of data humans had been producing daily since the early 21st century was mind-boggling and used words like zettabyte and yottabyte—quantities no human could fathom—to describe what humans produced daily. Since that time, a whole new field of study into digital archaeology had sprung up.

The Church employed the most digital archaeologists in the world, either directly or through their loosely affiliated subsidiary companies.

This is where Jade Palmer came in. Jade was a digital archaeologist.

Jade studied computers and the history of technology in college and became interested in analysis of ancient data, particularly scientific data, when she stumbled upon a long-forgotten paper by long-forgotten scientists. The scientists were Paul Horowitz and Carl Sagan. The paper was, "Five Years of Project META: an All-Sky Narrow-Band Radio Search for Extraterrestrial Signals."

This was an extraordinary find. The common understanding was that no one did extraterrestrial research. That was the domain of kooks and conspiracy theorists. Except Jade now had proof that in the distant past, searching for extraterrestrial life was performed by well-known scientists. Jade shared her findings with Blake who was studying computers along with physics and astronomy. Both made attempts to figure out when and why this research had been shut down. They could figure out the when, somewhere in the 2040s or 2050s. They couldn't pin-point the why.

Both Jade and Blake were currently employed by the Church in some way. But Blake occasionally fantasized about working for The Company and maybe heading out to Astroll 2 with the goal of setting up a covert space telescope there.

Jade didn't want to leave Earth. She thought she could be of most use on the planet, even though the planet was getting... uncomfortable. Everyone mindlessly went through their days. She didn't connect with people other than Blake and Logan. She was there for their wedding and shortly after decided it was time to have her own child. So, she did.

She continued the tradition of naming in her family which was to pick a precious or interesting gemstone or material. She picked 'Ruby.' It was a close tie between Ruby and Rhodochrosite, her other favorite red mineral but decided against the latter because a five-syllable name was bound to upset the majority of people she would encounter who were generally lazy and likely to shorten it into an unflattering nickname.

There were also the household robots to consider. The robots worked best with two, three syllables at most. Longer than that and it was worth abbreviating one's name.

Jade was now living on her own with her baby daughter, but only down the road from Blake and Logan.

She named Blake and Logan her baby's uncles, but also named them as the people who would take care of Ruby if anything happened to her. Not that she thought anything would happen to her, but her own mother, as crazy as she was, raised her to always be prepared. And that meant having plans for worst-case scenarios. It wasn't a big deal. Just some legal paperwork.

Blake was in his comfy pj pants and went to grab a shirt.

When he came back, Jade was already passing Ruby off to him so she could take out her computer.

"Look what I found," she said as she was opening it up.

"Ok but shhh…. Logan is sleeping, as is this little one," he rocked Ruby to make sure she didn't wake up.

Jade nodded and plopped herself on the couch. Not really trying to make any less noise, she opened her old-style computer on the coffee table. She touched the screen in a few places and a text-based document appeared on the screen.

"What is that?" Blake said—careful to be quiet—as he didn't plop, but carefully lowered himself to the couch next to Jade, with a still-sleeping Ruby in his arms.

"Proof!"

"Proof of…?"

"Sheesh Blake… it's what we've been looking for. It's proof! It's an old journal that used to be published called," she squinted at the screen, "called the 'The Planetary Science Journal.' It looked like it stopped publishing around 2040. I found an archive of their papers and there are a whole ton of them on the old satellites that visited Jupiter, and Saturn, and Titan. Look how many papers referenced the Cassini-Huygens mission! I knew it was a real mission…"

Blake made a little scooching motion so he could get a better look at the document. He was still holding Ruby, gently rocking her. He continued to rock Ruby and read.

The document was an ancient-style academic paper regarding the interior structure of Saturn's moon, Titan. It was titled, "Exosolar Sources Responsible for Titan's Interior Structure and Dynamics as Revealed by a Further Examination of Cassini-Huygens Mission Data."

"It was submitted, but never published," Jade explained. "This never became public, and it was right after this paper, that the Church manipulated to have the space telescope projects shut down. A replacement for the old James Webb was already underway, and it was shelved. And then there was a decrease in published papers on exoplanets, too."

Blake heard what Jade was saying and tried to make sense of it.

"But why would one random paper…"

"Oh, c'mon Blake! You're the astrophysicist! If this was a paper with no real data behind it, it would have been dismissed as quackery and no one would care."

Blake thought about that. Jade wasn't wrong. The truth is what scared people and caused them to shut down information. But what about the possibility of something coming from outside the solar system was scary? It had been known for a long time that our solar system was bombarded by comets and bits that were technically from the outside. That's the assumption he made when he saw the title.

"Let me go put Ruby down," he said, walking over to the spare crib they kept in the corner of the living room for visits like this, "and then I need to read that."

Chapter 16

> Ruby <

They were in the Hub. A makeshift stage had been constructed in the space on the opposite side of the Nook. Three rows of chairs of increasing height were set up, and a large green screen was placed behind them.

One chair was slightly offset, distinguishing itself from the others. That was the one Ruby sat on. Off to the side and behind sat her uncles. Robt Plampton sat with them. As did Milo. The broadcaster wanted Milo, the second human to meet the aliens, to be present and answer some questions.

A chair faced all the rest. This one was presumably for the interviewer. Ruby didn't know who that was going to be. Not that she was intimately familiar with the news and would recognize them. People who wanted real information about events looked to PeopleWire, where anyone could provide accounts of events along with evidence of the account, like videos. "News" was synonymous with "opinion pieces to argue over" and was one of the lowest forms of entertainment and something Ruby never took an interest in. She was surprised they were interested in her. Her news was more appropriate for PeopleWire since she had a first-hand account, complete with video of the robots to provide.

Ruby was placed in her chair first by someone who said their name so fast that Ruby missed it entirely. All she caught was that they were a producer. A seemingly busy one at that. The producer was shorter than Ruby and not much older, but focused and moving quickly. She had short curly hair that bounced around in the low gravity. A mere milli-second after Ruby was in her seat, facing the right way, the producer had moved on to seating the next person.

The producer placed Ruby's uncles next but left a seat open. Then Plampton. Then Milo. Next, she placed another individual Ruby didn't recognize in that open seat. Lastly, she brought in Professor Coronik to fill the second empty seat. Then she went off to talk to the man who was setting up a camera suite.

Ruby looked back over her shoulder at the man she didn't recognize. She had the distinct feeling that this man and Professor Coronik knew each other and didn't like each other. Maybe it was because of the way the two of them were angled ever so slightly, facing away from each other. But wasn't that the producers doing? Or did they just nudge themselves that way?

"Ok, listen up, everybody! This is going to be a live broadcast. People back on Earth want the unaltered truth, and that's what we at World Insights always give 'em. Our viewers are lucky 'cause they never have to choose their news because we've chosen it for them. Keep it real, keep it fun! We're makin' history here, people! We'll be live in ten!"

Ruby was fully aware that while a communications signal was leaving Astroll 2 as it happened, it would be nearly 20 minutes before anyone on Earth received it. Not quite 'live' exactly. Live, but with enough cushion room to edit anything out.

"Now, does anyone need anything?" the producer finished with.

Ruby raised a hand slowly and peeked over her shoulder, seeing that she was the only one who did so.

"I could use some water," she said.

The producer nodded at an assistant who presumably rushed off to take care of that.

"Anyone else? No? Ok, so here's the deal. We'll be running the intro, and then Garrett Spradley will walk in and take his seat here. He'll be running things for the whole 30 minute spot and introduce all of you to the audience. Every three minutes there will be a 30 second sponsorship break. About 15 minutes in, we'll bring in the robots."

Ruby didn't know that the robots would be on live until this moment. Something didn't feel right about that. She wished she had talked to them in advance of this to make sure they were okay with it. But they were just finishing up their formal station tour.

"You'll know when we're live versus on a break by this light set here," she pointed to a monitor. "It'll be blue when we're live and green when we're in a sponsorship break. It will flash red for 10 seconds before returning to live. And will flash yellow for five seconds before a break. Remember… those breaks are only 30 seconds long. Not much time to do much of anything. Stay put during those breaks, please!"

She looked over at the guests. She approached Uncle Logan and tried to press his hair down. When it didn't stay, she frowned and moved to look over the other guests. To Professor Coronik and the mystery guest next to him, she produced a curt smile and nodded approval. When she reached Ruby, she said, mostly under her breath, "I wish we had had a little more time on your hair."

"What's wrong with it?" Ruby asked.

"Pulled back ponytails are not very sexy. No, they're not in right now at all," the producer said. "I can tell you have some really nice curls. Curls look great on camera. We should have taken that ponytail down."

Now it was Ruby's turn to frown a little. She didn't really care what she looked like. That wasn't important. What was important was telling all of humanity how wonderful these alien robots were.

"Three minutes, everybody!" the producer shouted and looked around at her crew to examine everyone's state of readiness.

That was enough time, Ruby thought, so she turned around enough to get the attention of Mr. Mystery Guest. They locked eyes for a moment, and just as she was about to ask, "Who are you?" she heard some people making a commotion at the front of the Hub.

She looked over and saw several people talking and waving their hands. They were clearly having an argument. One where she couldn't make out the words anyone was saying because they were still too far away, and the sound wasn't carrying.

Uncle Blake had stood up from his assigned seat and scooted out in front. He looked at Ruby. "Stay here," he said.

"Hey!" said the producer. "We only have two minutes before we're live!"

Uncle Blake held up a finger to indicate this would just be a minute. Ruby was trying to look to see who she recognized in the crowd.

As her Uncle Blake got closer, she realized she recognized Char—wasn't Char the one taking the robots on the formally planned and sanctioned tour of Astroll 2? Where were they if not with them?

Blake engaged and then jogged back to Ruby. He was smirking, so she knew the robots were okay.

"The robots," he was shaking his head, "are busy. Char couldn't get them to leave the Arcade."

"Don't they know they're on a live broadcast in about 15 minutes?" The producer looked like her head was going to literally explode. Possibly on a live broadcast.

"I could get them," Ruby said.

The producer shot Ruby the ugliest, freaking-oh-my-god-no-you-don't look that was possible for a human being. "Absolutely not!" she said. "You are our main guest. You *cannot* leave."

Ruby shrugged, sharing a look of comedic approval with Blake. "Ok, I guess. Maybe humanity will have to wait to meet the robots."

"Maritza!" shouted the producer. A thin figure appeared as if by magic from nowhere, having provided a tumbler of water on a little console table to Ruby's side.

"Please find those robots and tell them that Ruby has asked for them," the producer said.

Ruby was not keen on having her name used like that, but in this case, she wouldn't protest. In truth, she thought it was a good idea for the robots to be introduced to humanity with her there to help facilitate and interpret since she was certain that it would take a while for anyone else to get used to the literal way they spoke and processed anything they heard.

The lights were dimming in the Hub, Uncle Blake returned to his seat, and Ruby realized she never had the chance to ask the Mystery Guest who he was. He had remained silent so far.

Music started playing. Ruby couldn't tell where it was coming from. It sounded familiar. Whatever show this was, she had probably seen it once or twice and forgotten. The word 'live' was repeated in various tones and at various pitches in a not-quite echo effect.

"Here is your host, best friend to all humanity, Garrett Spradley," also came from the same source as the music.

Then a man sat in the seat that had remained empty until now. His hair was white but not from age, and it rose high above his forehead. He wore a flat blue suit with a collar and generally looked well put together. Ruby also thought she recognized him and decided she should probably pretend to know who he was.

"Hello humanity! Good morning, good afternoon, and good evening to wherever you are watching this from. We have an amazing special edition of Humanity and Truth, live, from Astroll 2. Many of you know Astroll 2 as the space station you've never heard of. We're half a billion kilometers away from Earth in the main asteroid belt, a place where humanity has been quietly mining the asteroids for more than 100 years. Click on the links to learn more!"

Ruby watched as he shifted from looking at one camera to another. Ruby had missed the fact that there were a variety of cameras set up. She was told to not even look at any, but only at Garrett, the interviewer. She wondered if he was nervous at all. This was historical news, even Ruby could appreciate that, and he seemed so perfectly pampered and articulate. So much so that it almost bothered her. No, not almost. It *did* bother her.

"I'm your host, Garrett Spradley and right now… wow… I am so pleased and privileged to be speaking with Ruby Palmer along with her close family, friends, and colleagues. The only way you don't already know about Ruby Palmer is if you've been in a coma these past two weeks. And even then, that was probably the first thing you were told when you woke up: That Ruby Palmer is the first human to, without any doubt, have made contact with intelligent alien life from outside our solar system."

Now, he looked directly at Ruby.

"Ruby Palmer. I am honored."

"Um, thank you," Ruby said.

"Everyone has heard the basics of the story, but not directly from you. Tell us in your own words how you came to meet these aliens."

"Alien robots," Ruby corrected. She wanted to be as careful as she could with her terminology. She couldn't imagine the implications of miscommunicating something to all of humanity.

"Yes, of course."

"It's pretty simple. I was in my ship, and one of them, well, captured me."

"Captured? As in kidnapped? Are the aliens hostile?"

"I guess you could say I was kidnapped, but no, they're not hostile. They were looking for something that they thought I had."

"Well, they kidnapped you. That's a crime here." He said it, but he said it with a weird smile that Ruby was unsure how to interpret. It certainly made her feel like she was saying something wrong.

"It's fine, really," Ruby said, trying to make sure that this didn't go in a direction she didn't want it to go in. She attempted to gloss over it. "Call it a mistake. But yeah, they took me in their ship back to their home world. They call it Location Zero."

"Location Zero!" he said in his best interviewer voice. "Now that sounds like a perfect vacation spot." He chuckled at his own lack of a joke.

Ruby didn't acknowledge it, whatever it was.

"Moving on," he said, "Tell us. What did the robots do to you?"

"They didn't *do* anything to me. They wanted to test my DNA, which is no big deal. But they couldn't, and while we were trying to figure that out, I realized they had some problems, and I helped them. And we became friends."

"They didn't try to dissect you?" He looked at one of the cameras and smirked while he said this, then turned back to Ruby. "We've all seen movies and shows where that's what aliens try to do."

Ruby remembered back to when that's what she thought was going to happen, and when even some of the robots themselves thought was going to happen. She realized this was one of those situations where she probably would be better off not revealing every single detail. Just the gist would be enough.

"No, they didn't. Of course, I wouldn't be here if they did!"

"And who created the robots?"

"They don't know," Ruby said. "That's what they're searching for. Archives that will tell them where they come from. Who made them."

"Interesting. Now, let's move on to some of our other guests." He turned to the Mystery Guest first. Ruby was a little surprised that that's all he wanted from her, but at the same time, a little relieved to not have an extended time in the spotlight.

Mystery Guest was sharp-looking in a way that oozed wealth. Not just wealth, but uber wealth. The kind of wealth that filled people with hatred. And it made Professor Coronik, prime connector of the wealthiest church in the history of religions, look poor.

"First, we are very lucky to have with us Pat Marsden of

The Company. Mr. Marsden, thank you for being here today. This is, for all intents, your space station…"

Pat Marsden!? Ruby had heard the name, but it was always just a name. A name that held a mysterious, shadow-like power that she could never imagine a face to go with it.

"Oh, no, no, it is owned in part by all the long-term residents here."

Ruby pursed her lips together. He wasn't telling the entire truth. The Company owned the station. Everyone who lived here over sponsorship age received a fraction of a share in the station. Enough to get voting rights at annual board meetings, but not enough to do anything else with. Ruby knew enough, mostly from overhearing others, that the only reason The Company granted a part of a share was so it could make statements like the one Pat Marsden just made in news interviews like this.

"But it is Astroll 2 that is the site of this historic event, it is the legal residence of Ruby Palmer, who will go down in history as humankind's first contact, and it is currently playing host to three of Ruby's alien robots."

Ruby wasn't sure how they became hers but wasn't going to argue that point. She was more in awe of Pat Marsden, who owned The Company. Although it was his mother who started The Company, he was brought up specifically to be its heir. Grade school students learned about The Company and him in a form of standardized civics and economics class. Given she lived on Astroll 2, she had an advantage that she already knew a lot about The Company, and what she didn't know, she could ask her uncles.

In person, Pat Marsden looked like anybody else, only with fancier clothes. Ruby wasn't too surprised she found him that way. Celebrity—any kind of celebrity—didn't impress her.

"Yes, of course," Marsden responded. "That is why I'm here. Well, I was nearby on a survey mission. You may have seen our recent press release. We at The Company are looking for a site to host Astroll 3, since Astroll 2 has been such a success. But to answer your question, I am delighted that

Astroll 2 and one of our residents are part of this historic event."

Ruby wondered if he was capable of remembering her name, or if he could only think about The Company and *his* space station.

Garrett Spradley looked directly into the camera and said, "We'll talk to Professor Lloyd Coronik, Prime Connector of the Church of the Blockchain, and get his reaction, right after this message from our sponsor."

The lights behaved exactly as the producer said they would. Ruby turned around to look at everyone else. She wanted to catch Uncle Blake's eye and see if she could telepathically deduce what he thought about all this, but before that could happen, she saw the 10-second indicator come on out of the corner of her eye.

Then she remembered that she wasn't going to be addressed next. She turned back and managed to catch Uncle Blake's gaze. She smiled. He frowned. Why was he frowning?

"And we're back! Now let's get the reaction of Professor Lloyd Coronik. As Prime Connector of the Church of the Blockchain, he is frequently making headlines. Most recently, with the Blockchain developed software, TERP, that's now responsible for 80% of the world's governments," he chuckled a little uncomfortably at that comment, but didn't pause. "Professor Coronik, welcome and tell everyone, how's that going?"

Coronik looked the most uneasy since Ruby had met him. Was that because of the mention of TERP?

"I thought we were here to discuss Ruby's robots…"

"Oh, we are, we are," Spradley said, not losing his smile. "But since you're here, we thought you'd give us an update on TERP."

Coronik took in a visible breath and said, "It's going well. We are working closely with the government's head of IT to work out any issues—"

"We recently broke the news of the backlog of issues, and wow—everyone was surprised!"

"Well, yes, and we've got our best teams working on it."

"You have plans to get TERP under control?"

Under control? Ruby made a mental note that she needed to research more about what they were talking about.

"Certainly. We have a team of people who meet daily to review and report on the backlog."

"And what about the team *working* on the backlog?" Spradley still kept his smile, but Ruby would have sworn that she saw some daggers in his eyes as well.

"Of course," Professor Coronik said and let go of the breath he was holding.

"But you're right, Professor Coronik," Spradley again faced another camera and renewed his smile. "We are here to talk about these remarkable alien robots. Is that what brought you out to Astroll 2? We understand that Church leaders rarely leave Earth."

"Well, this is an amazing historic event! As leader of the Church, I wanted to be here to help usher and guide humankind into this new era."

"What era is that exactly?"

"An era where we know for a fact that we are not the only beings in the Universe."

"Wasn't the Church involved in shutting down all forms of SETI research...?"

"Oh, that's an embellishment of the past. At the time, the Church merely thought that those funds were better suited to focus on many of the problems at home. And we were right and successful, as evidenced by the greener planet that we have had in more than 400 years..."

Ruby knew that was partly true. She knew that's what was taught to people. Earth was quite green, Earth's temperature was under control. But what she'd also learned from the communal expression hubs, outside any formal classroom, was that there were so many robots. And while these hubs had been the center of human social contact for almost 200 years, ever since the early days of the networked computers, they were not representative of the best humanity had to offer and had never been quality sources of factual information.

The interview continued like this. The next few minutes was little more than banal banter between the interviewer and Pat Marsden of The Company and Coronik. Ruby couldn't tell exactly, but it looked like Marsden and the Professor had some preexisting dislike for each other. She couldn't fathom why. They were both part of the mega-wealthy elite and were probably only suited to hob-knob with each other. From Ruby's point of view, they should be best of friends.

Spradley barely asked Uncle Blake or Robt Plampton any questions. "How does it feel to have Ruby back?" "Wonderful—we were worried, of course." "How does it feel to be manager of the station during this historic event?" "Exciting—and I thought I was going to go down in history for being the longest running director." There was another sponsorship message before and after this set of questions.

When the interviewer got to Milo, Ruby could see him sweating. But not in the broadcast. A view of the broadcast was set up in Ruby's field of vision. She surmised that an algorithm must be in place to filter out Milo's sweat and make the older Marsden and Coronik have less wrinkles and imperfections than they really did.

Ruby didn't appreciate the fakeness but was grateful on Milo's behalf that the whole solar system wasn't going to see how nervous he was.

"Milo Jenkins," Spradley said. "You are the second person to have met the robots. When you met them, you must have had a million thoughts running through your head. Tell us, what were those thoughts?"

"Well, I was happy to see that Ruby wasn't harmed."

"Was that your primary concern?"

"Yes, of course."

Ruby could now see that he was blushing slightly under the sweat, and noticed her own cheeks felt a little hot.

"Well, the two of you now have something in common… the first humans to have ever met aliens. That puts you both in a special category."

"I guess so," Milo said.

"And when the robots met you, were they friendly? Did they try to hurt you in any way?"

"Of course, they were friendly. I know Ruby wouldn't have brought them here otherwise."

"And we're going to have one more message from our sponsors, then I hope everyone is ready to see those robots up close!"

Once again with the lights, and the second they came on, the producer was shouting, "Bring them in!"

There was a commotion, but Ruby could still see SD and Disto enter the Hub. The producer and her assistant escorted them to the area right next to Ruby and lined them up next to her.

"The camera is over there. But don't look at it. Look at him."

The robots followed the arm that was pointing to Spradley. They continued to look in that direction, like statues.

Ruby wasn't sure if they were going to make it in time, but magically, with two seconds to go, the producer and her assistant were out of the way, and all of a sudden Garrett Spradley was saying, in a somber voice, "and we're back. With very special guests. Probably the most special we've ever had or ever will have on this show. And we are grateful that we are the first ones to bring you… the alien robots."

He surveyed them and a wrinkle formed in his forehead. He looked genuinely caught off guard for a moment, "Wasn't there a third robot?" he said aloud and then as if he was getting an answer directly into his ear, mumbled, "uh huh," and then "mmm." The wrinkle disappeared, Spradley's direct smile returned, and everything resumed.

The broadcast screen filled with the three of them. Ruby and the robots. She tried to keep a pleasant smile, but she was nervous. More nervous than when it had just been her.

"Ruby," he said. "Do you want to introduce your…uh, friends?"

Ruby exhaled the breath she didn't know she was holding.

94

"Certainly," she said, and at those words she became excited to do so. She had a brief moment to wish that she knew this was what she was going to be asked, so she could have prepared herself, but it was okay.

She turned towards the robots and hoped that they were relaxed and not nervous. Why would they be? They didn't have those emotions.

"This is Detailed Historian. We call him 'Disto' for short. Next to him is Swell Driver, 'SD' for short. Guys, say 'hello.'"

Disto and SD said 'hello' in unison.

"Very interesting names," said the Spradley.

"Yeah, and they can be a mouthful, hence the nicknames."

"And which one of these kidnapped you?"

Ruby was feeling a little more comfortable and confident. "Yeah, let's not call it that anymore."

"What would you suggest instead? It was a ride-share service?"

"To answer the original question, SD was the first that I met. It's his ship that first connected with me and my ship, *Apple Pi,* and it was also his ship that brought us back and is docked outside Astroll 2 right now. I know everyone has seen pictures of it by now."

"Of course," said Spradley. "And how do they communicate with you?"

"We are capable of producing the same sounds as you," Disto said. "We talk. We are capable of multiple modes of communication. A variety of methods. And we understand your language very well."

This threw the interviewer off. He obviously wasn't used to any guest exerting control in that manner. Ruby smiled.

Chapter 17

> Blake <

Blake checked the expected delivery time on his phone. The flowers would be delivered to Logan at his office shortly. It wasn't a typical flower arrangement. They were all fake. As much as Logan enjoyed them, real flowers released too much pollen and could interfere with his job as an odorist.

The Company hired Logan shortly after the wedding, so not only was their first wedding anniversary coming up, so was his at The Company.

He walked down the sidewalk, making sure to avoid straying into the lane devoted to delivery bots and drones. He had opted for an old-school smartphone instead of the communicuff or eye-piece that most people had. He admitted the eye-piece would have been nice. He could be looking up and multi-tasking. Plus, he knew there were walking lane assist features that would ensure he was going the right way—which he often found that he was not.

But nope. Old phone for him. Logan teased him about it sometimes and at the end of the day, kept an old-school phone, too, just to humor his husband.

Blake did look up to find the sign of the store he was looking for. There it was. The bakery called *Bake District*. It was one of the places they had randomly wandered into on one of their first dates, on a recommendation from his pastry-chef mom, who happened to know the best bakeries in every major city.

Blake could easily have ordered remotely. But he wanted to walk in, smell all the warm vanilla in the air, and make a decision based on that, rather than from images you couldn't grasp or experience. It was too easy to deceive customers through advertisements, no matter how many countermeasures were in place to prevent such shenanigans, so Blake made a point to try and go in person whenever he could.

This bakery still made much of their stuff from hand, so each item had its imperfections and to Blake and Logan, that was heaven.

As he walked in, the pleasant scent of fresh bread hit him, and he took a deep breath. This was anniversary gift part two. Part three would be his attempt to cook dinner. He had plans for that, too, but it would have to wait until later when he was home. For dinner, he selected a menu and let the AI make the shopping list, place the order, and arrange delivery. While he was out, a robot drone would deliver, and their household suite would take care of the items.

He looked around. Something was off. Admittedly, he'd only been here that one time with Blake, but it felt different. Blake approached the counter and figured out what it was. There was no one behind it.

A robot arm on a floor track, what he recognized as a standard retail model, detected him and moved over, "How may I help you today?"

"Where is the owner?"

The robot arm pointed to a screen and must have clicked something since the menu that was displaying changed to a scrolling set of words. Blake read the story. Apparently, the owner had a stroke, and his kids took over the business. The kids had made changes that allowed the store to continue to financially operate. They were not bakers like their father but hoped that automation could keep the place going. Then the text went on to thank their customers—calling a few out by name—for accepting these changes.

Blake didn't have another plan, so he would have to accept it, too.

He examined the offerings in the case. They were all perfect. Too perfect. Human hands were no longer involved in creating these. As if on queue, the back door opened, and another robot arm appeared with a tray of fresh biscotti. The first arm opened up the case, took out an empty tray, and the second arm placed the fresh tray inside, took the empty tray from the first arm, and returned to the back kitchen.

The cookies looked perfect. They smelled heavenly. But there was something off about them. They reminded Blake of plastic, toy cookies that kids played with.

Nevertheless, that was one of the things Blake selected. While the robot arm was collecting the pastries into a box, Blake's phone rang. It was Jade.

"Where are you?" she asked.

"That bakery I told you about," Blake said.

"Can you talk?"

"Ehh... In a minute I'll be back outside walking. Where are you?"

"Work. Well, I'm working. Ruby had a little fever so we're at home. She's watching some old cartoons and laying down in my bed."

"Is she okay? Does she need her Uncle Blake?"

"She's fine. Really, just a little fever. But she did ask for you and I told her we'd see you this weekend."

Blake smiled. Both he and Logan loved spending time with Ruby and talked about adopting their own child. Ruby was so... uncomplicated. She liked to play and pretend and play some more. If her toys gave her any problems, from needing power to breaking in two, she liked to solve it herself and never got upset over it for very long. And when she was done, she liked to snuggle up and make him read her a book. There was no stress, no worries. Only simple play stuff.

The robot arm now held out a white box tied with a string and made a soft chime indicating it was ready to pick up. Blake grabbed the box and smiled, a little sad that he missed the opportunity to not only say "thank you" but talk to the person who made the goods.

Box in hand, he left the store.

"Okay, I'm outside, headed to the metro, but I can wander a few more minutes before I need to head back to the apartment. I'm cooking dinner."

"Oh, that's right—anniversary. Your gift is on the way, I promise!"

Blake smiled to himself. He knew there was no gift on the way. Jade was the worst when it came to remembering birthdays, anniversaries, and such, and hence, was the worst when it came to giving gifts. It didn't bother Blake. He didn't need or want anything that he didn't already have.

"So, what's up, Jade?"

"Remember we talked about Astroll 2?"

"The space station? Of course." Blake used to fantasize routinely about carrying out some ridiculous covert plan to set up a secret space telescope but hadn't had those thoughts in a long time.

"That's where it's all happening," Jade said.

"All what is happening?"

"The research. I found it. I found the construction plans. One of the planned rings—it was never part of Astroll 1 and there's almost no detail. That was always a little sketchy. It was too much space for what it needed to do. Well, that's because there's a lot more going on there than what people know."

"How did you find that?"

He knew Jade so well, he could see the exact facial expression she was making while she said, "You know all you need to know. The important thing is I think that's where you need to go."

"Excuse me? You want me to go to the space station."

"No, I don't want you to go. Well, I want you to go, and I want us to go. But you know I could never get there with my background. But you and Logan could... heck, Logan already works for The Company..."

"...and I could get a job there easily, I know. But Jade, I'm not a working astrophysicist, remember. I'm an engineer."

"All the better. Look, I can… add some records for you. You'll get hired easily."

"We need to talk about this more. Later."

"Can I come over? I'd rather show you in person. Look—I'll help you do a little of the cooking, and I'll be out of there before Logan comes home."

"What about Ruby?"

There was silence for a minute.

Blake also knew his friend well enough that he knew exactly the conflict that was going on in Jade's head. She had refused to install the commonplace nanny bot system. It was also inexpensive, made for people with few options and resources. It was essentially a safe room for ages three and up. You deployed the plexiglass container in a room, and a robot arm and series of cameras and AI watched your child. You could always look at the child and interact over voice or video. The system monitored the child's heart rate and ensured that nothing dangerous happened. You could leave approved toys in there, and the system could even play educational videos.

It was approved by the government and had various doctor's seals of approval.

But Jade didn't like it. She ranted about how unnatural it was and how a robot arm and AI shouldn't be left to care for a child, and she couldn't bear to let it care for hers.

When situations like this came up, she reconsidered that decision and always came on the side of, "Crap, Blake. If she didn't have this fever, I'd just bring her with me."

Blake chuckled, "And she'd be picking at all the food I'd be cooking, not to mention the pastries I'm carrying right now that smell so good."

He thought for a moment. He did want to know more about Astroll 2, although he was certain there was no way he'd ever manage to get there. But something in the back of his brain told him it made sense. It was a corporate entity, far from any government. The perfect place and platform for advanced extra-solar research that wasn't allowed here.

"What about tomorrow?" he asked.

Jade sighed. "Okay, this can wait. I'm certain I'll be home with Ruby tomorrow, too. You can come here anytime."

"Great. I'll let you know. Give that little girl a kiss from her uncle. Tell her I'll read to her when I'm there."

"Thanks. She'll love that. She loves her Uncle Blake. Let me know when you're headed over, okay?"

"Will do."

"Oh, and Blake? Happy anniversary. I mean it."

"I know," Blake said. "Thanks." Then he broke the connection.

He had been wandering aimlessly throughout the call, and now he looked up. He was a block from where he needed to be to catch the metro back to their apartment.

Logan had tried to talk Blake into getting a job at The Company. The Company was one of the largest employers of people with advanced scientific degrees in the region. Every now and then, Logan would forward Blake an interesting job requisition that listed an Astrophysics degree as one of the qualifications, mostly related to the ongoing search for qualified asteroid candidates to mine.

Now Jade had jumped on the bandwagon to encourage him to also go work for The Company. Blake knew she wouldn't encourage him on a whim. He also knew that she understood how important uncovering scientific mysteries and picking up where humanity had left off—on the verge of discovery—was, to both of them. Blake sighed. He now had a bigger present to give his husband—the news that he would consider a move half-way across the solar system.

Chapter 18

> Ruby <

The interview concluded with more ridiculous questions like whether or not the robots wanted to visit one of the popular theme parks on Earth. The robots handled themselves admirably. Disto was the one who spoke the most. SD hardly said anything.

The last question Spradley asked Ruby was: "What now?"

"I'm…I mean, *we're*," she gestured towards the robots, "We are headed to Earth."

"Obviously," Spradley responded while smiling directly into the camera. "But Ruby Palmer, what's next for *you?*"

Ruby didn't know what to say. Her mouth hung open for what felt like an eternity before Spradley must have realized that her mind was a complete blank, and he chimed in with, "I'm certain you have more options than you can count."

And then back to the camera, he said, "I'm certain the whole world, everyone who is everywhere, will be watching what you do next, Ruby Palmer."

Ruby could feel sweat beads form on her forehead. The last thing she wanted was for everyone to be watching her.

"Thank you for joining us live for this special edition of Humanity and Truth. I'm your host, Garrett Spradley, and until next time," he paused for what must have been dramatic effect, "stay voracious!"

After that, the light that was shining on Ruby and all the other guests turned off. The overhead lights of the Hub turned back on, and the producer went over and whispered in the interviewer's ear.

"That's great!" Spradley said. "I don't think it's possible to have more viewers than that!" The whole interview had lasted nearly an hour, and given it took almost thirty minutes for the broadcast to reach Earth, they already knew from their office back home how many people were logged in and watching the interview.

Spradley stood up.

"Ruby Palmer, great to meet you," he held up his hand in a soft wave. "Professor Coronik, Mr. Marsden…" he said something to every other human there. He ignored the robots. She watched him glance at them, but clearly, he didn't want to talk to them any more than he had to.

Was this going to be typical? People on Astroll 2 seemed generally fine, especially after they heard the robots speak and realized how nonthreatening they were.

Uncle Blake came up to her, took her hand, and smiled. She was about to ask him what he thought of her performance, but before she could say anything, the producer came up to them, too, and started speaking.

"Okay, you should know, while that was live, once it finishes playing out on Earth, it's going to continue to be available to replay on our parent channel. Of course, you can watch it, but a word of advice: don't read the comments."

"Wait, you allow comments?" Ruby asked.

That was unusual. There was even a time when it was illegal. But those laws were overturned before Ruby was born. Reading comments was not something she did. *Most* people were savvy enough not to either. It was weird that they just told her not to, like they were deliberately trying to make her curious, dangling something in front of her that she shouldn't do.

She felt Uncle Blake squeeze her hand, as if he was reading her thoughts. The hand squeeze said, "you know better." Then he let go and walked away.

"Yes, of course. It's all about engagement through the communal expression hubs. The more engagement, the more advertising. C'mon, we've been doing this for literally hundreds of years."

Ruby shrugged. "Okay, I guess. I really don't want to see myself anyway, so I'm not going to watch."

And then she turned around, and Inny was there, talking to the robots. Not just talking to them but showing themselves video of the interview. They were all hovered around a tablet she was carrying.

Inny was giggling.

"Ruby, you all looked great on camera! I saw it live! And look… look how many pos reactions so far! Okay, this one's pretty bad…but the rest are totally pos! Everyone loves you! Can I interview you next for the portfolio I'm building? I'm taking a freelancers class through The Company's school."

Ruby looked. There were indeed a lot of pos reactions coming in. She hadn't heard exactly the estimate of how many were watching it live, but she could appreciate the uniqueness, and understood that everyone knew who she was by now. While she had been staying away from the news, deliberately, her uncles and even Milo and Inny had told her some of what was reported.

She suspected they were leaving out parts. Every celebrity was researched to death, and it was easy to find information on someone's whole life. Not that she had done a lot before the whole robot thing, so she couldn't imagine that there was much to gossip about in her case.

Her mom died when she was young. That was probably the most interesting thing about her. She since lived on Astroll 2 with her uncles. Big deal.

"What's this?" Disto asked.

"Oh! That's the best part! That's the comments section…" said Inny.

"No, don't show them that," Ruby reached for the tablet.

"Comments?" SD asked.

"Seriously, Inny… don't show them that."

"But that's the best part," she said. "Here, let me read some to you."

"Um… robots are cute… Ruby is cute… Professor Coronik is… uh, I'll skip that… oh here's something good, 'those robots are fake, my kids could have dressed up better…' um, okay, that was weird…"

"Inny, really. Stop."

Inny held the tablet and was scrolling down. She was frowning.

"Maybe you were right," and handed Ruby the tablet.

Ruby couldn't help but peek. She saw, "Ruby Palmer must die for bringing the alien invaders here!"

"Doesn't everyone know that Astroll 2 is fake? It's a TV show. They're in one of the abandoned movie lots in La-La Land. This isn't real."

And it went on from there. Every now and then, someone said something nice.

"Uncle Blake…" she looked up, trying to hold back tears. "We can't go there…"

He put his arm around her shoulder and took hold of the tablet, pressing the off button as he did.

The robots were all looking expectantly at them, too.

"What does this mean?" Disto said.

Blake was the one that answered. "You're going to learn that humans are, well, still learning how to behave."

"Can't they be re-programmed?" SD chimed in.

Ruby and Blake both chuckled, and he said, "I wish."

"You never explained how humans are programmed in the first place."

"Well, we're not 'programmed,' but we are educated." Ruby said.

Blake raised an eyebrow, and Ruby added, "Ok, some people are educated. Most, probably."

"What is 'educated'?" Disto asked.

"It means we learn information."

"Ah—and I remember—no ports," SD said, and Ruby

smiled, remembering the first time she had to explain that her orifices were not data information ports.

"Yeah. We read, we listen to others. And our brains need to assimilate whatever comes in to understand it. Frankly, it might be easier if we *were* programmed."

"Some people think we are," Milo chimed in.

Ruby had nearly forgotten he was there. She looked at his face and saw the red tones in his skin become a little more pronounced. Was he blushing?

"Several of the comments I saw alluded to that," Ruby said, frowning. "I don't understand people."

"It's okay, kiddo," Blake said. "I think we have a trip to get ready for, anyway. Professor Coronik is coming with us. SD, Disto, I hope it's clear that the best way for all of us to get to Earth is on your ship. Do you have room for all of us?"

"Yes," SD responded.

"Um, can we add some seats?" Ruby added. She looked back and forth from Uncle Blake to Professor Coronik to Robt Plampton. "They aren't exactly outfitted like our ships. They don't have seats." She pointed to the robots, "since they obviously don't need them."

Plampton said, "we can use the industrial printers to generate some. The mining operation has us loaded up with extra material, and even if we didn't, I'm certain The Company would let us use what we have on hand."

"How long will it take us to get there?" Uncle Blake asked.

"Get where?" SD asked back.

"To Earth," he said.

"To the third planet you had on your map of our solar system," Ruby added for SD and Disto. "The one with all the bios."

"From here? Only an appendage full of tics," SD said.

"A tic is roughly a second," Ruby translated for the rest of the humans listening in, "and an appendage-full, well, I think he means 'handful', but you know, they don't have hands." As she said it, she could have sworn she saw both Professor Coronik and Pat Marsden of The Company suppress a smile.

Milo whistled, "wow—that's fast."

"Fast?" SD said.

"Yeah, fast as in," Milo was clearly figuring out how to explain the concept, "opposite of slow... uh..."

Now, it was Ruby's turn to smile. She had gotten used to thinking how to explain terms she never expected to have to explain.

"Explain it mathematically," she said. "SD, you can calculate the velocity of something, correct?"

"Yes. The rate at which an object moves. It's the distance traveled over a period of time."

"Now if you have a certain distance, say, here to Earth which is," she looked to Plampton, "where are we right now?"

"We're actually on the close approach side. Roughly 300 million kilometers away," he said, and then in almost a mutter, "Spradley got it wrong when he said half a billion. Not right now, anyway."

"Ok, so, if you go 300 million kilometers in a few days," Ruby continued, "that's one speed. But if you can do it in a few tics, you're going faster."

"Ah," both robots responded in unison.

"And if it's a few millitics, it's even faster!" SD said.

"Correct," said Ruby.

"And what if you go a shorter distance in the same amount of time?" SD asked.

"We call that going slower. The opposite of fast."

"Opposite. We know that concept," Disto added. "Diametrically different. The reverse form of something."

"Yes," Ruby said.

"I am not familiar with that," SD added.

Disto proceeded to beep and chirp in his native tones. All the humans except for Ruby jumped back a step.

Ruby explained about their native language. It was the first time they might have used it around other humans besides her.

"They don't do it much," she said. "Disto and the others understand politeness, and to be polite, they speak our language as much as they can. But for efficiency, well—"

"I understand the concept of opposite," SD blurted out excitedly. "Near and far. Robots and Bios."

"Functioning and broken," Disto added.

"Yes, you guys got it," Ruby said.

"Planet and star," SD said. And then Disto and SD shot back and forth several more examples.

"It's like a three-year-old Sebastian, but double," Uncle Blake whispered into Ruby's ear. She remembered that time, when he was a toddler, and yeah, that might be why she had the patience for this. She had patience for him, too, when he was at those stages of asking a ton of questions. Often the same question over and over and over to reaffirm what he heard. It was normal for toddlers. The difference here is that once the robots got a concept she explained, they got it. There were no repeats.

"Well, I think we have a trip to prepare for," a voice boomed from behind Ruby. Professor Coronik made sure a large number of people who were still present stopped their own conversations to hear him speak. Headed to Earth was indeed what was next for all of them, and Ruby was happy to focus on that and not answer any more uncomfortable questions like what was next *for her.*

Chapter 19

> Ruby <

They were using a mini-R-pod to ferry all the passengers from Astroll 2 to SD's ship. It was Milo's pod, *Pecan Pi*, but *Key Lime Pi*—typically piloted by Harmony Ortiz—was standing by.

Milo had just arrived from delivering SD and Disto first. Next was going to be Ruby, Uncle Blake, and Coronik.

A news crew was nearby to watch. In the last several days, things on Astroll 2 had become frenzied. Even more than they had been.

Robt Plampton had to welcome more people on the station than he was comfortable with. The station typically held 2000 people at any given time. Roughly 5% of those people were temporary guests.

That was the ratio the station was designed to handle, with a little allowance for overflow. Temporary guests were given smaller quarters, had to eat at the mess hall, and most importantly, didn't have all the training that permanent residents had. And they were not expected to behave the way residents were expected to. But with only 100 or so at any time and plenty more residents, there were plenty of people to make sure that the guests didn't do anything, well, dangerous.

The station could hold close to 1000 guests if it had to. But that was only intended for emergencies—like if a ship that was nearby had to evacuate. Not that any individual ship produced by humans to date was able to carry 1000 people—the upper limit to the outer solar system was still only 100—but there could be an ultra-rare scenario where several of those had an emergency at once.

Right now, there were close to three times as many guests as Astroll 2 had ever handled before, and it was putting a strain on everything. The second Plampton realized it was going to happen, he ordered more supplies—which had arrived on the transport that carried Coronik—but still. It was annoying.

And now, as many of these guests as possible—who were mostly some form of media or press—were jammed into the viewing area of the hanger with their various forms of cameras and recording devices.

Uncle Blake was saying goodbye to Sebastian and Uncle Logan. Mostly for Sebastian's sake, they decided it was best for them to remain on the station. The plan was that Ruby and Blake would help Disto and SD find what they were looking for and then return to Astroll 2. No one was sure exactly how long they'd be gone, but Ruby promised Sebastian they'd be back before Sebastian's birthday.

"You haven't taken me to the arcade since you've come home," Sebastian said to Ruby, tugging on the sleeves of her jacket. She hugged him.

"I've been just a little bit busy, you know."

"I know… but I thought you were dead. You owe me."

Ah, the logic of a seven-year-old. Ruby hugged him again.

"Ok. You're right! I owe you. I'll bring you something from Earth. How 'bout that?"

"Where on Earth are you going?"

Ruby pressed her lips together, "I'm not exactly sure. Maybe Greenland." She really didn't know their ultimate destination on Earth yet, so she blurted out the first place that came to mind.

"You know green is my favorite color!" *Ah, the non-sequiturs of a seven-year-old.*

"And you know Greenland isn't green?"

"It's not?" Sebastian said with a true sense of shock and wonder.

Ruby smiled and placed her palm against his cheek instinctively. She remembered it was the same comforting move her mother did to her. Sebastian closed his eyes, smiled, and leaned into it. He opened his eyes a few moments later when she pulled her hand away.

Milo came over, "Pre-check complete. Are you all ready to get on board?"

Ruby looked at Uncle Blake and Coronik. Both nodded. Then they all followed Milo onto *Pecan Pi* and took a seat.

"Interesting naming convention for your little ships," Coronik said.

"It was way before my time," Milo said as he closed the hatch behind them. Things were tight, but there were four seats, and everyone took theirs. Ruby sat in the co-pilot's seat and assumed this role, touching the console and examining the ship's systems.

"Mine, too, but Milo—haven't you read the plaque?"

"Oh right," he said.

"Plaque?" Coronik asked.

"It's on the hangar. It says, 'We commission these ships in the name of our favorite foods that we will never eat since we chose to live out on this monstrosity.'" Ruby said. She knew that underneath, it listed the first hangar chief and crew members, along with the first pilots. At the time, there were only two. The team had grown to a dozen active pilots, with more on Astroll 2 who could serve as co-pilot or come up to speed in an emergency.

"That's why are they all named after Pie?"

"Not Pie. *Pi*."

"Excuse me?"

"Pi… the number."

Coronik nodded but uncertainly said, "Well yes, I've heard of pi. It's a very important number."

Both Ruby and Milo allowed themselves small smiles. Uncle Blake didn't. Ruby had noticed that Uncle Blake had become very tense and extra silent when Coronik was around in the last day or two.

She wanted to ask what was up but was waiting for the right time.

Milo took his place in the pilot's seat and examined his console. Looking on, Ruby knew that he was waiting for the all-clear from the hanger crew. With so many people to clear out of the hangar, it would take a few minutes.

"Everyone strapped in?" Milo said. He turned around to make sure he had nods from all. As many times as Ruby had piloted *Apple Pi*, she never had this many people at once. She was usually tugging a piece of equipment around, that's all.

She wasn't sure if she would be comfortable with this many eyes watching her every move. Even if they were friendly eyes.

She also wasn't sure she liked the silence coming from behind her. Uncle Blake wasn't the chattiest of people. He was one of those 'only speaks if he has something to say' types, but she was surprised he didn't have more to say to the Prime Connector of the Church of the Blockchain.

So far, her interaction with Coronik had been pleasant enough. He seemed to genuinely want to help.

But a desire to help didn't completely jive with everything she had been told about the Church over the years to include how controlling they were. They were also unpredictable, exemplars at blaming others, and masters of the guilt trip.

Although could this be his attempt to control the situation?

"We're about to launch," Milo said. Ruby confirmed from her console.

He touched a button or two, and the ship lifted off the platform and a small propulsive force pushed them away from Astroll 2.

SD's ship was straight ahead. The large monstrosity already had its mouth open, waiting for them.

This was now Milo's third time piloting into the alien ship, and he seemed completely unfazed—like it was his 300th.

"It'll take a few minutes. Heck, it will take longer to get to the ship than it'll be to get to Earth," he said. Then shook his head and said under his breath, "amazing!"

"Sure you don't want to come with us?" Ruby said. "I'm sure that would be okay."

Milo ran his fingers over his head, not going through any hair because he kept it nearly shaved in a fade. His eyes were aimed at the floor, and then he looked up and locked into hers.

"I'd love to," he said, "but I still have a day job." He smiled.

Ruby smiled back and shrugged.

"Can we get Astroll 2 up on the monitor?" Uncle Blake asked.

"Sure," Ruby said. As co-pilot, she could take care of that. She pressed a button on the console, and a small display opened on top of the main window that showed what the cameras out the back end of *Pecan Pi* saw.

It was Astroll 2, looking directly at the spin axis and the hangar ring. The hangar door was already closed so they couldn't see inside. From this vantage point, Astroll 2 looked like a flat disk. They could see the rest of the "A" ring as well, since it had a larger diameter than the one they just exited. And that was about it. Everything behind that ring was obscured from this point of view.

"Thanks," Blake said. "It's been a while since I've seen it from the outside. I was curious."

Ruby smiled but watched as Coronik leaned in to take a good hard look as well. As if he was actually looking for something. He frowned a little and leaned back. All without saying anything.

"Okay, we're about to get taken in by SD's ship," Milo said.

They could feel the clunk of metal on metal as the mouth of SD's ship connected with the bottom of *Pecan Pi*.

There was no way for them to detect whether or not the air around the ship was breathable—mini-R-pods weren't equipped with sensors since the expectation was that the only two operating conditions would be out in space, where they weren't needed or on the hangar of Astroll 2, where a team of people were responsible and knew whether the air was breathable or not.

Milo pressed a button on his panel, "This is Milo on *Pecan Pi*. Are you ready for us?"

"Yes," Ruby heard SD's voice, "you may exit your ship."

Everyone unbuckled, but only Milo got up, went to the hatch and opened it. Outside, Disto was waiting.

"Greetingsss!" he said. Ruby smiled.

Blake exited first, followed by Coronik. Ruby was wondering why they were both taking tentative steps and realized that this was their first time on the ship. On an alien ship.

She had already gotten so used to the robots and their ship and things that she kept forgetting that this was new to everyone else.

"Welcome," she said. "To SD's ship. No name, like we name our ships. We just call it SD's ship."

"Actually," Disto interrupted, "it does have a designator."

"Oh?" Ruby said, "I didn't know that! See," she looked at Blake and Coronik. "I'm still learning, too."

"What is it?" she asked Disto.

"I can't tell you."

"Why's that?"

"Well, I could," he said. Then he made a screeching noise that had all four humans covering their ears.

"What the hell was that?" Coronik said. It was the first time he had spoken since they boarded *Pecan Pi* and left Astroll 2.

"That is the designation for this object," Disto responded. "Every object has one."

"...and there is no translation," Ruby nodded her head in understanding.

"Correct," said Disto. "Now, let me bring you to the control center and primary cabin."

"Wait," Ruby said, "We need to get Milo prepped to go back to Astroll 2."

Disto rolled over to the wall and connected to a console. A moment later, he disconnected and rolled back and said to the group of confused humans, "but he can't go back. We're already at the third planet from the star."

"What?" all four humans said simultaneously.

"Yes, I just confirmed with SD. He believed the instructions were to go to Earth right after you were all on board. Accordingly, he did."

Professor Coronik ogled in disbelief. "Then that means…"

Disto sounded proud, "We're here."

Chapter 20

> Ruby <

"Where are we, and I mean, where *exactly* are we?" Ruby asked.

"At the stable point between Earth and its moon," SD said. "Standard parking location for any planet with a single moon."

Ruby understood. There were typically five such stable points in any two-body system. They were called "Lagrange Points" named after some ancient mathematician or physicist or something or other. Whatever they were called, they were points of gravitational equilibrium between the two large masses—the points where the gravitational pull was equal.

The point in between two bodies, where they were right now, was called "L1" for short.

"Between Earth and the Moon is not a good place for us to stay too long," Coronik said. "There are several other objects here, most notably our E2M comm relay."

"We could go to L2?" Milo offered. L2 was the 2nd of the five points. It was on the other side of the Moon.

"Sure," Ruby said and shrugged her shoulders. No one else seemed to object. "SD, you know the other stable points?"

SD brought up a map on the main screen. It showed animated representations of the Earth and Moon and dotted lines that Ruby believed represented the gravitational field, given she recognized the five Lagrange points as blinking yellow dots.

"That one," she said, pointing to the L2 point.

"Understood," SD said.

"Please be careful," Blake said. "We have many valuable assets around Earth and the Moon."

"The ship is able to detect and avoid all objects," SD said.

Ruby got the sense that this didn't make Blake feel any better.

"Approaching destination," SD said, "and there is an object there. Putting on screen."

"What is that?" Ruby asked.

They all stared at what looked like a platform with some kind of pointing array on top.

"Oh wow," Blake said, "I know what that is… that's the ancient James Webb Space Telescope. One of the last of its kind."

"It was only supposed to operate for five or ten years," Blake continued, "but they were able to refuel it, so its mission carried on for nearly 40."

"I can circle around that point in space. That is another stable trajectory." SD offered.

"Uncle Blake, where are we supposed to land?"

Did Robt Plampton or the head of The Company give them any indication of who they were supposed to contact when they were here? Did Coronik know? Surely as head the Church?

"And do we have another problem? Can this ship land in an atmosphere?" Milo added.

"Ruby, I have never landed on a planet before," SD said.

"Never? I thought you flew all over the place!"

"I have, but I've never landed. Just docked."

"Let me ask you this… had you not swallowed my ship the way you did when we first met, what were you going to do to collect your sample?"

SD was silent.

"You would have come to Earth, right?"

"Correct. Bio Muck Ball 23 is the label in our database."

"And then what?"

SD was silent.

Ruby pursed her lips. This was disconcerting. How could he not recall?

"Well, never mind, I guess," she said. "But we still need a way to get to Earth. And a landing spot... assuming we can land."

Unlike the way they used the mini-R-pod to help them transfer from the ship to the station, the mini-R-pod wasn't suitable to enter Earth's atmosphere, either.

"What about Legacy Station?" Uncle Blake offered.

Everyone, well, at least all of the humans, who all knew about Legacy Station, looked at Professor Coronik. When they saw all the humans looking that way, the robots followed suit.

"Yes, we can dock with Legacy Station. And disembark from there."

Legacy Station was wholly owned and operated by the Church. It was a space elevator station. The first and only one of its kind, and up until now, only members of the Church were allowed in or on.

It touched down on the planet in the middle of the Atlantic Ocean. All parts of it were considered sacred, but the geo platform was the liftoff point to get to the Moon.

The Church claim that non-members couldn't use it was for liability reasons. They claimed it was all part of keeping things on the Moon functioning, and really, the only use was to service that. It would be too expensive for the average person to make use of.

But everyone was certain that Church members made regular pilgrimages for the view.

"I will call and make arrangements for us to dock at the station. Will you be able to navigate us into a geosynchronous orbit?"

"A planetary synchronous orbit," Ruby explained. "The 'geo' just means synchronous to Earth." Every planet or moon had their version of 'synchronous'—the orbit that made it look like you were moving with the ground, or hovering over it, depending upon your point of view.

SD beeped to indicate he understood, and as he maneuvered the ship towards a synchronous orbit, Ruby watched Earth grow bigger in the viewscreen. If you'd have asked her a month ago if she thought she'd be this close to Earth anytime in her future, near or otherwise, she wouldn't have been able to stop laughing long enough to say, "no."

But there it was, growing larger by the second. The planet of her birth. The planet of her mother's death. And a place she'd thought was always part of her past, not her future. Especially not her immediate, imminent future.

Chapter 21

> Swell Driver <

Swell Driver wasn't used to having passengers on his ship. He never would have thought it would cause him distress, but it was. He was used to a typical trip consisting of him and his computer console, and that was all.

At least he could still communicate with the computer console in his native language. He would have been even more irritated if he had to deal with multiple levels of translation, such as the computer translating, and then he having to translate back.

In fact, he couldn't recall the last time even a robot was on his ship. Ruby, of course, was only recently a passenger, and he was thankful for her. She was a wonderful friend.

But he wasn't certain how to process all the other humans he had encountered. He wasn't built for that kind of processing.

Why couldn't he pretend they were unusual versions of robots? Reframe his viewpoint a little bit. That certainly would have been easier.

Maybe he could imagine they were robots like AT. Unusual and unlike any robot he had encountered before.

He thought. As he thought it, something didn't feel right. Like what was happening wasn't really true, even though he knew it was. He had clear memories all the way back to—

"There it is!" one of the humans declared.

SD turned his top chassis to see the human designated 'Blake' point at his screen. He looked where the pointing was occurring and saw the object he had recently detected. They called it a 'telescope.'

When SD didn't recognize the word, even though there was a translation for it, he asked the computer what it was.

Disto overheard, and had moved closer, obviously similarly curious.

"An object meant for observation."

"That isn't very specific," Disto responded. SD noted that he was also conversing back in their native chirps and beeps and was glad for that for a moment.

The humans were busy studying the object. All of them were interested in it for some reason.

To SD, it was just an object that was in the way.

"Make sure you don't disturb it, SD, please," Ruby had said.

"Acknowledged, but," SD said, "what is the significance of this object?"

"It's ancient!" she said. "Uncle Blake? You know a little more about these things."

"It was from the time that astronomy and astrophysics were respected scientific endeavors," Blake responded, "and not just a means to an economic end." SD saw that Blake had narrowed his eyes and glanced at the human designated Coronik. He wasn't sure what to make of that gesture or if it was one of the random and uncontrollable ones he learned that humans made all the time.

If he had not been a driver, he could have been a Zoologist. These beings were interesting, and it would have been an engaging position. But not so much that he was willing to violate his programming. He was a Driver. His programming dictated that, and that was okay by SD.

"I wish we could park and get a closer look," Blake said.

Ruby looked at SD, "Could we?"

SD asked the computer to compute a trajectory that would have them sidled up to the side of the object. The computer responded with the appropriate modifications to their current trajectory, which would have them go around it, around the Moon, and rendezvous with the station that was recently asked for.

"We can do that," SD said. "For how long will we hold position?"

Ruby looked at Blake, who said, "Wow. I, um, this is an amazing opportunity. I don't know. An hour? Does anyone mind?"

No one objected, so SD made the necessary modifications, and a few tics later, they were parked alongside the telescope.

"SD," Blake said, "Do you have the ability to take pictures?"

"Indeed," responded SD. "We are recording."

"Thank you so much. Did you know this is now a museum?" Blake added.

SD wasn't sure if he was meant to know that or not, but he answered honestly. "I did not."

"I didn't either," Ruby chimed in. "A museum? Like one people can visit?"

"There was a plan for that," Blake said. "A long time ago. After the one and only manned visit, there was an expectation of more. Technically, this is a historic monument, but one that no one visits. Probably a good trivia question for some trivia night someplace."

"I'll try to remember that," Ruby said.

"See look," Blake said pointing at the telescope on the screen, "see the secondary sunshield that was added to keep the mission going after the first twenty years?"

"How do you know so much about this?" Disto asked. "I was under the impression that human's knowledge of the galaxy was limited."

"Yeah, Uncle Blake. How *do you* know so much about this?"

SD was certain he heard Ruby emphasize a few words in her question.

"Can I talk to you on the other side of the room or cabin or…whatever this is?" Blake said, facing Ruby.

"Sure," she responded.

The two of them walked to the back of the room, and while they lowered their decibels, it was still in the range of what SD was able to detect. He wondered if the intent was for him not to do such a thing, but it was his ship, after all. He was entitled to know everything that was happening within it.

"I had been meaning to tell you," Blake said.

"Tell me what?"

"About my real profession," he said. Quickly, SD had the computer tell him what 'profession' was.

"I wasn't just a homemaker," Blake was already continuing. "I had another purpose on Astroll 2."

"I was starting to wonder," Ruby said. "I hadn't thought too deeply about it before, but while I was gone, I had a lot of time to think and… never mind… what *do* you do on Astroll 2?"

"Extra-solar astrophysics research."

"But… but no one does that."

"We do. Quietly."

"But the Church…"

"…doesn't know. And can't know. That's one reason why I came, to make sure they don't suspect anything. To make sure this whole situation doesn't unearth a can of worms that *has* to stay underground."

"You've got more to tell me, don't you, Uncle Blake."

"Yes, but it's going to have to wait until we're on the ground."

After that, the two of them joined the other humans. Milo and Coronik were still looking at the viewscreen.

If human's outer chassis turned colors like his did, it might have been a high six threats, a color Ruby called "orange," indicating that she was frustrated. Although she was exhibiting many of the outward signs of Bio frustration. Maybe that's why humans didn't color like robots did, because their emotions couldn't be captured so discretely.

He also saw Disto, and suspected he was doing his best to remain polite.

> Detailed Historian <

Disto was doing his best to remain polite, but he was agitated. He was anxious. He was a lot of things, but he was activating his patience algorithm, the one that returned the result that it was 'okay to wait.' It was the one that produced ancillary data that concluded that he had waited this long, so waiting a little longer was fine.

He watched his traveling companions watch an inanimate object out in space. They could see one side of it, illuminated by the host star.

SD provided him access to the second computer console. Typically, ships were designed with one Driver in mind, but occasionally there was a second, and so there was a second terminal. The humans called it co-pilot.

Either way, it kept his circuits mildly distracted. He was scanning all the emissions over a wide range of the electromagnetic spectrum that Ruby told him were in common use by her kind. There were emissions coming from the Earth—the humans primary residence. There were also emissions coming from Earth's moon, another object in the system. Also, from Astroll 2, several ships that were moving throughout the system, and of course, all the spacecraft that were created by the humans and left all over their solar system. Their system was polluted with them.

"What are you doing?" Professor Coronik asked him. All the humans had been staring at the object in space, but it was possible that the object out there wasn't interesting to all of them.

"I am scanning," Disto replied. "There is a lot of… overlapping signals from a variety of objects."

He examined Coronik's face as he responded, observing movement over one of Coronik's optical sensors. Humans had a substance they called 'hair' on their faces—all humans had this on their faces, immediately above their visual sensors. Some of Coronik's hair moved.

"Indeed," Professor Coronik said simultaneously with the

movement. "What type of signals?"

"They are predominantly from the orbiting planets in this solar system," Disto said. "But there is a lot of... noise... I think is the appropriate word or description. It is interesting that you can function with all of this out here. Is it all necessary?"

"Well," Coronik began, "You ask a good question."

"Do you have a good answer?"

The hair above Coronik's optical sensors returned to their initial position and then moved down some more. His face took on a similar one that he'd spot on Ruby occasionally. It indicated some form of displeasure. Disto couldn't compute why this simple question would produce that result.

"Well, as the head of the Church, I am generally unconcerned with these matters."

"Unconcerned does not mean you lack the knowledge."

"Well in this case, I'm trying to say that this is not my area of expertise. So no, I do not have a good answer for you."

"What *is* your area of expertise?" Disto asked. He was generally curious. "Heads" of anything would typically be chosen based on a certain level of experience and expertise, would they not?

Disto waited for Coronik to continue, but instead of responding, Coronik turned away from Disto. Maybe he had a circuit terminate abnormally.

"Well, speaking of signals," Coronik said, loudly, and grabbing everyone's attention, "I think it's about time I made contact with the station. To let them know to prepare for our docking and put SD," he said SD's name as if it was hard to remember, "in touch with the right people to coordinate that activity."

This soothed Disto's circuits that remained anxious for him to get on with his search.

"I will initiate a communications link for you," Disto said. "On what frequency?" It became a simple question once Ruby was able to understand what frequency meant. The robots used the term slightly differently than humans, and they both agreed that humans were the one who used it inaccurately. Humans, apparently, on average, didn't think of all the electromagnetic radiation as the same thing. They divided it up into different domains.

Nevertheless, Coronik did not respond to the simple question.

"Coronik," Blake said, "What is the communications frequency?"

"Well, I, uh," he said.

"You what?" Blake asked.

"I have people for that," he said.

Disto watched Blake look at Ruby, then at the floor, and shook his head and Disto could tell that Blake was also doing his best to remain polite, although he couldn't fathom why there was reason for anything otherwise.

"Disto," Blake addressed him, "I assume you can modulate a tone at 59.61 GigaHertz."

"Yes."

"Please do. They'll respond with a tone, and then voice communication will be possible," Blake said.

"How did you...?" Coronik asked Blake an incomplete question.

Blake gave Coronik a look from re-shaped optical sensors, one that Disto was unfamiliar with, and didn't say anything else until a human voice came through the system, "Legacy Station. This channel is for special use only. Who's there?"

Silly Insane Humans

Chapter 22

> Ruby <

"This is unacceptable," Coronik said. "I am the Prime Connector—"

"I'm sorry, Prime Connector," said a voice that emanated from an image on the screen in front of him. "But we can't authorize you to dock."

Ruby, along with her uncle, Milo, and the robots, could do nothing but observe what she imagined must be a supremely embarrassing moment for Coronik.

"Which government has instructed you to do this?" Coronik said. He was seething. He was much better at seething than Ruby had ever been.

"Uh, well, all of them. Except for the unicameral congress of the Federates States of Micronesia. They apparently voted to allow it. But sir," the voice said, "It's not *really* the governments."

"What do you mean?" Coronik asked, beads of sweat visibly forming on his forehead.

"It's *you know who*," the voice said, almost whispering so someone or *something* wouldn't hear him, "it's the AI. It's TERP."

Coronik looked over his shoulder, and Ruby wondered why TERP was a subject of the conversation about them getting to Earth. She thought about asking, but Coronik didn't give her a

127

chance.

"Ok, Micronesia it is then," he said and swallowed.

Ruby did not know much about this Micronesia place. In truth, she knew very little about the geography or politics, for that matter, of Earth. It was something she had avoided at every opportunity.

"I don't suppose Micronesia has a landing site?" Ruby asked.

"Well, Micronesia is a group of islands in the Pacific Ocean," Coronik said. "And no, they do not."

He looked at SD, "unless you can land on water?"

"This ship will interface with substances that have a surface tension of... I'm not sure how to define it for you," SD said. Ruby wasn't sure that Coronik's question required an answer but smiled at the fact that SD tried to answer anyway.

"What do we do?" Ruby asked. "Head back to Astroll 2?"

Coronik dismissed his underling on the video and leaned back, and steepled his fingers.

"Did they give a reason why?" Uncle Blake asked.

"Well," Coronik started, clearly uncomfortable, "The AI, TERP, it has, well, not been able to process the concept of alien robots."

"Okay, someone please explain what's going on with this TERP? If it's some AI, can't it just be turned off?" Ruby felt bad the second she said this out loud and looked at the robots to see if they were insulted.

Coronik's jaw tightened. Ruby looked at Uncle Blake, who answered.

"Similar to the AI that The Company provided to Astroll 2 and The Company's ships, the Church provided its own AI to the various governments of Earth. An upgrade," Uncle Blake said that last word while making quotes in the air with his hands.

"I know that part already," Ruby said. "That doesn't explain why everyone is so tense about it."

"Well, it was years in development and just as long in negotiations. We've had the best engineers and team the

Church has to offer supporting this project," Coronik said, straightening himself up in a way that suggested he was giving a sales pitch for the millionth time. "It wasn't deployed until a few months ago, and it was…"

"Initially deployed in secret," Uncle Blake finished when Coronik couldn't.

"Well, no," Coronik stood and looked insulted. "It was done entirely legally, and all the documentation was available…"

Uncle Blake waved him off and continued the explanation. "If you followed some of the more obscure news then yes, maybe you would have known. I *have* been following it," and as he said that he shot Coronik a look that Ruby couldn't identify, "and it was only supposed to work on the governmental financials—it was supposed to balance the budgets of some of the most convoluted and complicated governments the world has produced."

Uncle Blake paused and continued to look at Coronik who looked like he wanted to hide under a rock.

Coronik's right eye twitched slightly as Blake continued, "It was done under *your* recommendation and persuasion. When the AI was deployed, TERP decided that there were more issues than just the budget. Then it decided it should run everything."

"What the…?" Ruby said.

"Yes, there are AIs running the governments of the world right now." Coronik's back slumped a little as he said this, and he made remarkable eye contact with the floor.

Ruby put a hand over her mouth as she tried to understand what this meant. She felt young and inadequate and, if she was being honest with herself, uneducated. She was, of course, aware of government, but once again, not something she paid much attention to in school and not something that she felt affected her life much on Astroll 2. Companies, not government, were in control usually. Weren't they? Government… well… what did they do?

Her whole image of Earth was shifting. She had dreaded

returning, even for a short time, even for a visit, for so much of her life but she now recognized that her impressions of it, everything, was probably totally off.

Part of that realization made her want to go and see what it was all about. Part of it scared her.

She looked over at the robots. Robots, AI... was there a difference? The AI that Uncle Blake and Coronik were talking about—it probably didn't have a body and maybe that's the thing about it that made Ruby a little queasy...

"Where is this AI located?" Disto interrupted her thoughts. Ruby didn't realize the robots were listening in, but of course, they were.

The question was quite obviously directed at Coronik, and Coronik quite obviously didn't have an answer since his mouth was open and nothing was coming out.

Finally, someone spoke. It was Uncle Blake. "You've hit on one of the main problems, Disto," he said. "The TERP algorithm doesn't have a central processing location. It transfers around the global network."

Coronik looked relieved—too relieved—that someone answered for him. Something about that added to her sense of queasiness, so Ruby decided to be a little more direct with her next question. "Explain to me, Coronik, what's TERPs problem with these robots?"

"Well, your robots are... well, they have a level of sentience. I think TERP must see that as a threat to them," Coronik said. "And it's Profess—"

"Yeah, okay, *Professor*. But there are so many robots on Earth already, with all varying levels of AI," Ruby said.

"Yes, but none are sentient," Coronik said.

"Maybe we should consider them people in a robotic shell," Ruby offered.

Coronik scoffed, "Well, that is utterly ridiculous. No one will accept that man can be... man-made." He resumed the straight back and air of superiority that he donned since she first met him.

Ruby squinted and, knowing that she was on to something,

straightened her own back. "There are plenty of people who have artificial components, right? Well, what if a person was fully replaced by components. What are they?"

"Well, they are people, because they were born people," Coronik answered confidently. "But…" he trailed off as he looked around the room of humans and robots looking at him. "I'm not going to argue. We all want the same thing here, to get to Earth. Let me see what I can do."

> Ruby <

Coronik was in touch with the Deputy Commander of Legacy Station. Legacy Station—wholly owned and operated by the Church of the Blockchain—had to give Coronik much more than the time of day. They begrudgingly gave him the forms for the permits that were required to dock and continue on to Earth, not so much based on Ruby's argument that Coronik passed on, but more based on Coronik's not-so-subtle reminder that he had ultimate authority over their employment status with the Church.

"I am receiving a…very large…file," SD said.

"How large?" Ruby asked.

"It's 1024 hunks," SD responded.

"A hunk is what they call a Gigabyte," Ruby added before any of the other humans asked.

"I thought it was going to be a simple form," Ruby said. "SD, can you display it?"

SD tapped his console, and a form came up for all to see.

Ruby took control so she could scroll up and down. "You've got to be kidding me," she said.

"The robots don't even have most of this information," she muttered. The form asked for fairly normal stuff—for a human. Birthdate, place of birth, gender—with all 12 options—eye color… and a host of other identifying features that could typically be autofilled from an image.

"Can we say, 'not applicable' to 90 percent of this?" she asked. She had SD transfer it to her communicuff so she could start filling it out. She had Pippa present the form in a hover screen over her hand.

"I'll help," Blake said. The two of them sat down on the 3D printed chairs. SD positioned himself next to Ruby so he could see the form as well.

As Ruby scrolled down the ephemeral image, SD exclaimed, "Oh look! There is contact information for a help center."

"Yeah, let's not do that just yet," Ruby suggested. "'Help centers' aren't always that helpful." She saw Blake and Milo both nodding their heads in knowing agreement. Coronik didn't respond at all. Ruby assumed that he likely had people who had people who filled in his forms.

Ruby responded 'not applicable' as much as she could. Any question that asked for a physical location she wrote in 'Location Zero' even though it didn't help autofill any of the other fields. 'Planet' wasn't a requested field anywhere.

She knew this was a general problem—she had it when she was doing school stuff. All the forms, while the school allowed for distance education to be completed from anywhere, even off planet, the forms hadn't been updated to account for the fact that someone's location was off planet.

To that end, she had used her grandmother's address a few times and hoped that her school didn't attempt to deliver any packages to her grandmother. Once, she needed a set of equipment for a laboratory class. Rather than have it shipped to her grandmother and have to explain that she needed it out on Astroll 2, Ruby decided it was easier to drop the class.

After several minutes of constructing creative answers to the questions, Blake let out an, "Oh no."

Before Ruby could ask what that was about, he continued, "This is the wrong form. This is an immigration form," he said.

"But the robots aren't immigrating, they're visiting," Ruby responded. Then she said, "Oh no," too.

Coronik got back in touch with the station, but this time demanded to speak to the station's Commander. He successfully communicated that it was the wrong form, received endless apologies, and was promised that the right form was on its way over.

Unfortunately, the next form wasn't any shorter. In fact, it was longer. They requested even more information for someone who was visiting.

While Ruby was re-inputting in her grandmother's address, Blake said, "We should go visit her while we're back."

Ruby looked at Uncle Blake and scrunched her face. "I barely know her."

It wasn't that Ruby didn't want to see her grandmother. Well, if truth be told, it was exactly that. She occasionally received letters from the woman, who was clearly in a facility for a reason. The letter would typically start out addressed to Ruby, but somewhere would transition into a missive with her daughter, Jade—Ruby's mother.

"Couldn't we see your parents instead, Uncle Blake?"

"They're a little harder to nail down from day-to-day. You know that, kiddo."

Since Blake and Ruby's mother had been childhood friends, he knew Ruby's grandmother better than Ruby herself did. Blake's own parents, who were retired and volunteering with the Paramount Global Pantry—a professional volunteer organization that used chefs, foodies, and nutritionists and sent them around the world. They knew and clearly remembered Ruby, as evidenced by their digital postcards—often from places Ruby hadn't heard of. She was thinking that maybe if she had paid attention to where they were each time, she would have a better idea of the geography of Earth. Blake's parents were pastry chefs. Well, his mom was a pastry chef, and his father was a famous chocolatier and they went around the world training people—and robots—in pastry and chocolate making.

They were technically retired, and as such, busier than ever as restaurants around the Earth called for their services to better train the people who should have been trained, but normally let the robots do their work. No restaurant kitchen was complete without at least a few robots involved in food prep and cleaning. Serving, too. There were humans that supervised. Or rather watched TV and listened to music in the backrooms, occasionally checking in on the robots. The robots rarely made mistakes, but Uncle Blake always said that sometimes the mistakes were the fun parts of restaurant dining. Ruby shook her head back into her original question. She would much rather see the pastry chef and chocolatier than her own whack-a-doodle grandmother. But she sighed and left her grandmother's address in the form. *Pastry chefs give you cookies. Whack-a-doodle grandmothers give you odd, squinting looks that remind you of your mother.*

"Done," Ruby eventually declared. She pressed a button, and the computer did an autocheck. It passed. At least she managed to fill out all the required fields.

"What next?" she asked.

"SD should transmit it to the station, and I will have my people submit it," Coronik said. "I'm afraid that it is going to need to be copied to a regulatory agency of the United Nations responsible for global migration."

Disto squealed. "I get it!" he said. "I know the word for this. It's called bureaucracy. Yes! I learned that concept and this is exactly it!"

"Why are you so excited about it?" Ruby asked.

"It means that bits are moving, individuals are getting the information they need, and our activities are being coordinated amongst the different enterprises. Our actions are formalized. It's order amongst chaos!"

"Wow, Disto, I had no idea... back at Location Zero you seemed pained by your version of a bureaucracy system."

"That's because our system has degraded. It has flaws. You are well aware of these since you helped us fix some of them. But as any system grows, it needs order else everything will disrupt into chaos."

Ruby had never thought about paperwork as something that brought order to chaos. She thought about all the times it gave her headaches. All the times she was asked for information that could easily have been pulled out of a database. All the times that she was asked for information that had nothing to do with the task at hand. She thought about the times that she needed help, and whoever or whatever entity she was dealing with couldn't help when the situation was unexpected or didn't have an immediate protocol. That was probably the worst.

But she was always given the riot act about needing a digital 'paper trail.' Even though paper was an ancient relic, the term was still widely used and understood.

"I have received confirmation that our form has been received," SD said. And after a few moments, "…and a new form. Am I interpreting this correctly? It's asking for us to confirm that we've received the confirmation?"

Ruby looked over one side of SD's chassis and Uncle Blake looked over the other.

Blake said, "that's exactly what it looks like. It looks automated, too. I thought there were supposed to be humans handling these forms."

Professor Coronik coughed.

Everyone turned to look at him.

"Well, our AI might have gotten involved in some of the other bureaus as well…"

"There's more," SD said. "I'm getting additional requests… there are many."

Ruby read the headlines of the digital forms as they made it to SD's computer. There was one titled 'Declaration of Intent at Destination' and another 'Proof of Vehicle Ownership.' There was even a 'Non-Disclosure Agreement for Time Spent on Legacy Station.'

"All this to get back to Earth?" Uncle Blake said. The question was aimed straight at Coronik. "Would we have to do this even if the robots were not on board?"

"Well, no…" Coronik responded. "This must be because we're carrying aliens. The AI is trained to recognize them as foreigners and must be designing a new process on the fly. We've never had aliens before."

Chapter 23

> Ruby <

Now, it was a waiting game. With all the paperwork submitted. Did they have any food on board? Ruby was getting hungry, as her growling stomach could attest to.

The robots didn't need food. They needed power, which they could get from the ship.

Disto was plugged in and drawing power. Ruby watched and listened in as Coronik attempted to have a conversation with the robots to try and understand the root power source of the ship.

She knew it was a futile ask going in. She was not even sure how much the robots really even knew. But it was entertaining to watch, nonetheless. If AT was active, maybe he would have been able to explain more. Ruby put her hand over the pocket that held AT and realized that when she was filling out all those forms, she only mentioned SD and Disto. She thought about saying something but figured as long as AT stayed in his powered down and shrunken state, she could have been carrying a rock as far as anyone was concerned.

"We are not traveling at the moment," Disto had said when Coronik asked what they used for power.

"Well, I did not ask about propulsion, I asked about power," Coronik repeated. There were some beeps and chirps as the robots tried to parse what Coronik was saying. Ruby still didn't recognize any of them. Only a highly trained ear might someday be able to understand the robot's native language. Ruby was certain that this ear did not belong to her.

"Power," SD added, "is a force multiplied by speed."

Ruby squinted one eye as she called up memories of her basic physics class, and at least in her head agreed that that was the correct way to define power.

"But what supplies that force?" Coronik asked, believing he was getting somewhere.

"The ship," both robots replied in unison.

Coronik crossed his arms in front of his chest, holding one elbow in one hand and his lower face in his other. Ruby saw his shoulder rise and eyes close as he took a deep breath.

When his shoulders lowered, he opened his eyes and removed his hand so he could speak again. But before he said anything, he turned to Ruby.

"Can you assist?" he asked.

"I can try," she responded. "What exactly do you want me to do?"

"I want to understand what powers this ship and what powers them. Maybe if they were willing to share some of their amazing technology with us… you understand where I'm going with this."

Ruby smiled gently. "Professor, I don't think they are programmed," she air-quoted that last word, "to give us any of their technology. I'm also not sure any of the robots here understand any of their fundamentals."

"Oh?"

"Remember I was on their home planet for almost a month. It seems that whoever or whatever created them and gifted them with their tech is long gone, and they don't have solid memories. They know what they're programmed to know and not much more."

She looked over at the robots who were all watching her. Well, SD still had his face-screen trained on his console.

"Now can I ask *you* something," Ruby was feeling emboldened by the fact that they were out here, and she was surrounded by her peeps.

Professor Coronik's eyes shot up. "Certainly."

"Why are you really here?" she asked.

"Ruby," Uncle Blake reached out an arm, but Ruby turned to him and tried to telepathically say to him "it's okay, I got this."

"I want to help," Coronik responded.

"Really? How so? And how come you haven't been able to simply get us permission to land at your station. It is *your* station, isn't it? And you are the Prime Connector?"

"We are subject to laws just as anyone else is," he responded.

"But I thought you helped make the laws," Ruby looked him straight in the eyes, and then briefly caught Uncle Blake smirking proudly in her peripheral vision. "The Church is responsible for 90% of the algorithms and programming that is used everywhere, right?"

"That is an exaggerated number, but I understand your point. Let me talk to my people on the station again. Privately."

Ruby squinted at him and turned around to roll her eyes. Privately.

The only way to give him his requested privacy was for everyone to go down to where *Pecan Pi* was stowed. They did so. SD stayed with Coronik, but on the condition that if he overheard anything, he would keep it private.

Ruby was surprised that this was sufficient for Coronik but didn't question it.

While they were down in the hangar, Milo occupied himself with inspecting *Pecan Pi*.

"Something isn't right, Uncle Blake," Ruby said. Disto was perched by her side. She didn't mind if he overheard anything she had to say.

"Once we're on the ground, I'm sure everything will be fine," he said. He had a certainness about him that confused Ruby. It was the way he was standing, the stillness of his hands, the easiness of his breath.

"Uncle Blake…" she began. She got caught up in looking

at him. In his narrow gaze, she saw someone slightly different than she'd known all her life. He didn't seem like a simple homemaker, or a caretaker, or an average Astroll 2 resident anymore. The revelation that there could be things still to uncover about him... well, she was still processing that fact.

She didn't know what to ask him.

"Astrophysics? How did I not know this?" she said, finally.

Uncle Blake smiled. "I'm sorry. That was intentional. No one could know."

"Does Uncle Logan know?"

"Somewhat. The general concept, yes. The specifics, no."

"And what are those specifics?"

"Well, I did go to the same University with your mother. But I studied physics and astrochemistry. I was starting a research project but it was shutdown before I could even get a good start. That university was one of the last places to be touched by the general degradation of science."

He looked to make sure Milo was still occupied.

"I found work easily enough. Especially since your mom helped."

"My mom? How? I thought she was a computer programmer?"

"Yes and no. She was a computer archaeologist. While you do have to be a programmer to do that work, she wasn't programming for the sake of programming. She was really an archaeologist of our modern digital times. Not a big field, considering how much data there is to go through."

"You told me she was a programmer..."

"I know. I'm sorry. If I had told you anymore, I know you would have been asking more questions. Questions that I wasn't prepared to answer."

"Excuse me," Disto said, "but what is an archaeologist?"

Ruby chuckled. "Ironically, it's not too different from what you do," she said. "They look at history and artifacts and such."

"In this case," Blake added, "digital artifacts."

"Did you guys work together?" Ruby asked.

"Yes, of course," Blake said. "At the end of the day, we

were really both interested in the same thing. We were just involved in two different ways. We both wanted to know more about our galaxy and Universe. We wanted to know about alien life and planets around other stars.

"She had uncovered some not-too-old research and long story short... I found out exactly who was still actively working on that. The Company. So, I started working for them, too."

"I am curious," Disto asked. "Were you aware of our planet?"

Blake looked at him. "That's the interesting thing. No. Your homeworld, Location Zero, is well within the range of our ability to see. Yet we only see your star and a large planet. Around the orbit you describe...*nothing*."

"That is interesting," Disto said. "I wonder why."

"Before we left Astroll 2, I stopped by the," he gave Ruby a glance, "telescope observatory." Ruby's eyes went wide. *I didn't know we had an observatory!*

"I used the location information you provided," Blake continued, "and confirmed. We really can't see your planet. We should be able to. I can only think of a few reasons why that should be and only one of those reasons seems probable."

Ruby got a chill down her spine when the reason occurred to her, too.

"Someone is preventing them from being seen," she said softly.

"Uh-huh," Blake said, nodding.

They were all silent for a moment, and then Blake said to Disto, "Who made you?"

"As we've expressed," Disto responded, "we don't know. I sincerely hope we can find out while we're here."

"Why here?" Blake asked.

"Odds," said Disto. "We have tested many other species from other worlds. Your world is fairly close, and teaming with life."

"Why didn't you test us sooner?" Blake asked.

Ruby was about to ask the same question. She was a little puzzled at herself for not asking it earlier.

"It's quite simple," Disto said. "We didn't know about you before. We had no records."

"Then how did SD wind up finding me? Where did his programming come from to get here?"

"As you know Ruby, all the programming comes from The Core. We have the special projects branch—"

"Yes, yes, but really… where did it come from?"

She watched Disto's coloring change to one of mild embarrassment.

"If I knew the answer to that, Ruby, I might know the answer to a lot of my questions."

Before anyone could ask anymore unsatisfyingly unanswerable questions, the lift opened at the back of the hangar and Professor Coronik appeared.

"We can dock," he announced. "But there are some conditions."

Chapter 24

> Ruby <

"SD is currently maneuvering us into the correct location," Coronik said, "based on a set of instructions my people have provided."

Ruby was still angry. She didn't like the deal that Coronik had made, but there was nothing she could do about it.

The deal was that they could dock, depart, and head to Earth, but the robots would temporarily be in Coronik's custody. Not as visitors but as property.

Ruby didn't like it one bit. These robots had more in common with a toddler than what was typically an Earth-created robot. They were sentient. She had no idea how that was or why that was, but she knew it when she saw it, as could any reasonable human.

To compare them to property…. She was fuming.

Blake had his hand on her upper arm, to help keep her calm.

"I'm staying with them," she said to Blake. "Something isn't right about this."

"Let's get on the ground first. Then we can sort this out further."

Uncle Blake wasn't wrong. There wasn't much they could do here. In fact, there wasn't much they could do anywhere. But she wasn't sure what difference being on the ground would make. She felt a new longing to be back on Astroll 2, where she felt she had some control, but that control was probably an illusion. Although a comfortable illusion was preferable to this uncomfortable reality.

SD interrupted her thought spirals when he said, "We've been asked to wait." SD had a direct communication channel open that allowed him to communicate to the individuals manning the station at the end of a rope.

But SD kept the Legacy Station on the viewscreen as well. It was another ring-like disk, similar to Astroll 2, but it was one single, solitary ring. However, it looked like it could have been designed by the same space architect. It was slightly more than 100-meters in diameter and was spinning. The tether could be seen beginning in the center of the disk and then disappearing as it dropped down towards the Earth. A climber was parked and appeared like it was ready to descend at any time.

Ruby wondered if they took the climber down to Earth, would that mean whoever was manning the station was stuck until the next climber arrived back? She searched her brain for what she might have learned about Legacy Station, but like most of her time in school, if it was about Earth, she didn't pay much attention. Her lack of interest disappointed her now.

As if reading her mind—or maybe she heard Disto ask some questions while she was lost in thought—Professor Coronik started to explain:

"Well, once we're on the station, we'll board the 'climber' that will take us down to Earth. You can see it here," and he pointed to the near center of the rotating disk. "Typically, this station has a crew of about 30 individuals, and there are escape pods if they had to evacuate in an emergency. We will attach here," and he pointed to another location on the disk.

"That is not the same location as was communicated," SD said.

Milo stood near SD and nodded hesitantly. He opened his mouth as if he wanted to say something, but then bit the inside of his cheek instead.

Professor Coronik cocked his head and said, "Well, yes, of course. You misunderstood how I was pointing."

Ruby didn't understand how anyone could misunderstand a point but let it go.

"Legacy Station began operation only sixty years ago, even though it had been under development for most of a century. The basic physics and engineering of creating such a structure had been studied longer than that," Coronik said.

"What is the purpose of this structure?" Disto asked.

"Well, it's a stopping point to or from the Moon. It's also a data transfer point between Earth and the data centers located on the Moon. You can see the antennas here," and he pointed some more.

"Those are the Earth-facing antennas," Uncle Blake stated.

"Yes, of course they are," Coronik said. "They are also part of the overall transfer mechanism."

Ruby wanted to chime in and disagree with him. Those were clearly the voice and small data transmitters. The primary data to and from Earth was built into the tether itself. What Ruby couldn't figure out is if Coronik was deliberately trying to mislead them or if he genuinely didn't know how his space station worked.

"Data centers?" Disto said. "For storage? Off-world? Like us?"

"Yes, but for different reasons," Uncle Blake said, and Ruby wondered if he, too, was picking up the fact that Coronik's answers were incomplete or flat-out wrong. "For a generation or two, nearly 200 years ago, we built what we used to call data centers on Earth. They served a need at the time but were terrible. Data centers generated a lot of heat, and it was killing the Earth. Eventually, we got a little smarter and moved them to the Moon."

Coronik nodded. "Exactly what I was going to say."

> Detailed Historian <

Disto considered what the humans were saying and looked to Ruby.

"Heat?"

"You know temperature?" Ruby tried to help. Disto knew what temperature was but still didn't understand the importance. Temperature was how you could tell if a robot was functioning well or if it was processing too much nonsensical data.

Temperature was how some agents knew that a robot was not being truthful. Or whether or not they were trying to process something.

Temperature was also one of the metrics he used to know how well his components were functioning.

"Yes, I know temperature," he said.

"Well, heat is what gets transferred from something hotter to something colder. There is a whole class I had to take, not to mention pilot training… right Milo?"

"Oh yeah. I would say all pilots are experts in heat transfer."

"We also call it thermal energy," Ruby said. "And so—"

Coronik interrupted, "Well, surely you can understand that it's not good to have all that thermal energy dumped onto our planet." He was clearly trying to stay involved in this conversation. There was no reason to talk over Ruby, but he must have concluded that what he needed to say was more important. Something about this human Disto didn't like, but none of his circuits could compute why. So far, everything he had done had tried to help them.

"And this is not a problem for your moon?" Disto asked.

"No. The Moon has no atmosphere and no natural life that can be harmed by that change to the environment. The heat can simply radiate away," Coronik said.

"Interesting solution to your storage problem," Disto said.

Disto considered for a moment why the robots hadn't developed a solution that was closer to home. While no one knew who constructed his planet, Location Zero was certainly constructed, as opposed to the standard way it was understood that planets were created. Organically.

"I wonder why The Core didn't create a moon for storage," Ruby half-asked.

"I don't know if we can be certain it didn't," responded

Disto.

"What do you mean?" Ruby asked.

"Perhaps it was created. Maybe it didn't work. Or maybe there weren't enough resources left over after creating Location Zero. Maybe it was considered. I will ask The Core and various agencies when we return home, especially if that answer isn't in whatever we find here."

Location Zero had no moon. Disto was certain of that fact. And to his historical knowledge, Location Zero had never had a moon. But he knew his own historical knowledge had limitations, and so he could be less certain of this second fact. He didn't know how much he could trust his own historical knowledge.

When Disto was initially constructed, he was given the base algorithm, which covered his general purpose: analysis, discovery, and preservation of history. Then, he was programmed with specific algorithms to carry out this purpose.

He was also provided a base set of knowledge of historical events. But then he got involved in the special project, attempting to find other historical data. Ever since he joined that special project, the rest of his historian duties fell to the wayside. He had not been collecting more recent facts about Location Zero and the robots.

"And these events happened before you were born?" he looked at Ruby.

"Yup," she said. "I learned about them in school and from reading and watching vids."

"Who teaches you?"

"Teachers? Historians? A lot of historians write books. That's how they tell people about history. Or vids... Vids are much more popular than books."

Disto's circuits were tingling. "Can I see one of these vids?"

"Sure! I can bring something up on my communicuff. What do you want to learn about?"

"Anything!"

Ruby looked at him and then smiled before she said, "Pippa, show us a vid on the origin of the word 'robot.'"

"Certainly," answered Pippa's voice, "but do you want to respond to your incoming messages? The number of unread messages has started to exceed—"

"No," Ruby interrupted. "Later. Please show the vid."

A holoscreen appeared and a human girl, who, to Disto's limited exposure to humans looked a little like Ruby, but not quite, appeared, and moved her limbs in a way Disto didn't understand.

"Hi, everyone! Welcome back to HiAllCoTe, the History of All Cool Technologies. I'm Tianna Tutor, your friendly technology historian here to tell you today about the origin of robots!"

The screen changed and a series of images flashed by, followed by some text. When Tianna Tutor reappeared, she started speaking again:

"Ok super-fans, this one goes out to Samera Huynh who asked about robots and where they came from. For that, we're going to have to go back to ancient times—the early 20th century and talk about a play. Yes, a play!

"This guy, Karel Capek—I have no idea if I'm pronouncing his name right—wrote a play that came out in 1920 called 'Rossum's Universal Robots.' It is the first time anyone had ever used the word 'robot' that we know of.

"But these robots aren't what we know of as robots today. These things were artificial biological creatures. They looked like humans—which makes sense given it was a play, like I said, and humans were playing them. But they were intended to be artificial creatures. Created differently than human beings."

Immediately after she said the words, 'human beings,' a sound effect was added—that nearly translated to the word 'transform' in Disto's native language—and an image popped up to replace Tianna briefly, and then she was back.

"The play was a huge success, translated into lots of languages, yada yada. Not too long after that, robots became a mainstay in science fiction.

"But that's all the fictional stuff. I know Samera was asking where real robots came from. As we all know, science fiction breeds reality. Since lots of people try to make sci-fi real, there was a lot of interest in building robots. At first, they were simple machines with motors that could automate tasks."

As she spoke, images appeared on the screen with her.

"Like these large industrial robotic arms that were popular in the late 20th century."

She went on to describe more of these devices, created at the hands of humans like Ruby, to do a variety of tasks.

As the video continued, Disto was more interested in watching Ruby who was watching the video with intense interest.

> Ruby <

Ruby was watching the video with interest. Intensely. The history and origin of robots was yet another on the long list of things she had little interest in before, but now she was captivated.

Robots had killed her mother. This was the statement she had told herself over and over and over… until she met SD and Disto, and the other robots of Location Zero, and had started to reflect on her life and what she thought she knew. She had begun to realize and accept that maybe she had misunderstandings about her past.

The most captivating point that she didn't know until now is when in the video, Tianna Tutor went on to explain the robotic laws.

"Before we get to about the year 2100 which was a watershed time, let's go back to the 1900's. There was a very influential science fiction writer named Isaac Asimov. Decades after he died, there was a lot of controversy over whether or not people could continue to read his work because it was known that he did not treat women well… but part of his legacy… in his science fiction… were what he called the three laws of robotics. They were laws about how robots could not harm humans.

"For the longest time, these 'laws' remained in the domain

of science fiction. Robots were not sophisticated enough—any harm would be obviously mishandling and misprogramming on the part of the humans. There were huge controversies over this in the 2030s, about the time that self-driving cars—early versions of the Dynamic Autonomous Vehicle that used primitive AI—were becoming popular.

"But when robots crossed a certain line of sophistication, the robot laws were passed, and they were based on Asimov's laws. Everyone who programmed a robot had to prove that these laws were incorporated into them.

"Which is how we know robots are safe today. Of course, there can still be accidents. There are always a handful of incidents that really are accidents…"

Ruby felt as if Tianna was talking directly to her and not to a mass audience of unknown people.

"But as long as the robot has its certification to operate based on the Robot and Artificial Intelligence Laws of 2098, things move on. Since then…"

The video went on for another minute, but Ruby was no longer listening. She had intended to think about this when she got back, but she'd been so busy talking to everyone about her experience and worrying about the robots, she hadn't thought too deeply about how to investigate or learn more about her mother's death.

The moments on Location Zero came back to her. Realizing that everything wasn't what it seemed to be when it came to her mother. Her palms began to sweat, and her teeth clenched.

She didn't realize she was making a face until she looked up and saw Uncle Blake's look of concern.

"Ruby?" he said. "Are you okay?"

"Tell me again what happened to my mother." Ruby said without delay.

"It's been a long time since you asked. In fact, I don't think you ever asked since we talked about it after it happened. It was a power surge—right in the middle of her operation. The backup power generation equipment failed. The whole city was affected. It was deemed a solar flare-initiated blackout."

"Robots didn't kill my mother?"

"No! Oh my god... is that what you've thought all these years?"

The tears came like a tsunami. Ruby couldn't hold them back. She didn't care that everyone was watching, she didn't care that she was being more vulnerable than she could usually tolerate being, and she didn't care that everyone could see her nose getting runny. Uncle Blake wrapped his arms around her, and she cried for a while. Ruby hadn't cried like this in a *very* long time.

Chapter 25

> Interlude <

It is commonly believed that a single human, who went by the name Benjamin Franklin, was the person to discover electricity. And while, for some unknown reason, his efforts are the ones that made it into popular lore, humans had been aware of electricity and more specifically, electrical charge for thousands of years before Franklin was born.

They were indeed aware that they could induce static electricity—a phenomena resulting from the imbalance of negative and positive charges in objects.

The ancient Greeks knew this. They knew that if they rubbed animal fur against amber, they could pick up other pieces of glass. They were also aware of electric fish that swam in the Nile River.

As the centuries passed, as Benjamin Franklin lived and died, humans learned more about electricity and started to give names to the particles they discovered were responsible for electric charge.

Indeed, as humans came to rely more and more on electricity to power their devices and their world, many became very concerned and familiar with the fact that while electricity could provide power, it could also kill their devices. Many humans continued to remain ignorant of this fact, scratching their heads when their device suddenly died after they walked across the carpet and touched something they shouldn't have.

As humans moved into space, many continued the study of electricity and brought the concerns of electrical charge with them.

They knew that for two human-made objects to touch in space, they needed to be at the same electric potential, or find a safe way to come to that, so an electrical charge didn't damage one or the other.

By this time, humans knew that if two objects were at different electric potentials, that shock was caused by electrons rushing to get from the more crowded object to the less crowded object. Electrons had no compunction about being polite, so they would rush to do it the instant they could, hence a spark!

These days all human-made spaceships had a special device to dissipate and prevent any ESD—Electrostatic Discharge—event from disrupting operations.

This was so common that no one thought about it.

Which means no one thought about it when SD moved in to connect to Legacy Station.

> Ruby <

"Ten meters," said Milo. Milo was SD's anointed co-pilot, to help keep the other humans informed of their progress. They had an open communication line to the station's main operations center as well.

Milo was staying quiet, doing his job, and seemed to be completely in his own zone. Ruby appreciated his professionalism. It certainly gave her less to worry about.

SD had flipped the ship around, so the ship's rear could make contact. Legacy station had a hangar, similar to Astroll 2, but much larger. The service hatch was the most compatible, and the station would use its emergency expandable antechamber to make up the difference.

It was better than using the mini-R-pod to shuttle people, everyone agreed.

"Five meters," Milo announced.

"Adjust your trajectory by point-five degrees not-yaw," said a voice from the station.

Earlier, they had worked out what roll, pitch, and yaw meant. The robots had equivalents for these terms, of course. In fact, the robots had more terms. While the humans described these three movements, using positive or negative angles to account for how you could move one way or the other, the robots had completely unique names. To make the translation, instead of saying a negative number as in "move five degrees in the negative yaw direction" or "move negative five degrees," the humans agreed to call the six angles of rotation: yaw, not-yaw, roll, not-roll, pitch, and not-pitch.

"We don't have 'negative,'" Disto had said after conferring with SD to try and understand what the humans were saying.

"But how do you describe anything that is," Ruby wasn't sure what she was trying to express and waved her arm in a circle to try and force some words out, "anything that is less than zero?"

"How can there be anything less than zero?" Disto said. "Zero is nothing. It is the lowest amount or lowest level. It is the origin point."

Ruby considered that. An origin point was always determined by someone. It could always be set. If there was an expectation of a negative quantity, you could move the origin to be at that lowest point. Is this what the robots did?

But how could they account for infinity? This was starting to hurt her head.

She knew that their sense of time came from when they were brought online. "But how do you describe the time from before you were born?"

"Against the master reference clock," they said. Ruby had learned about this during her stay on Location Zero. The Core maintained the clock, and everything was referenced to it.

Ruby did the math. The clock had been running for nearly seven hundred years her time. When she tried to ask about what happened before that, she got blank stares.

She tried to ask Disto about it. "Is it possible your planet and all the robots are only 700 years old?"

Disto didn't dismiss the possibility, but he simply said, "that's what I'm trying to find out."

The mystery gnawed at Ruby, too, a human with no stake in the problem. She tried to imagine that if she had a stake, how committed to it she would be. She was trying to sympathize with this robot.

"Five degrees, not-yaw, complete," SD said.

"Slow your rate of speed," was the next command overheard on the communications link.

"Speed reduction confirmed," SD said. They were already moving incredibly slow, Ruby thought. She was a little surprised that SD could continue to reduce it further.

"Two meters," Milo announced.

"Okay, we're going to link with our arm…" the voice said.

This was part of the prearranged procedure to ensure that they could connect. Since they couldn't connect port to port or hatch to hatch, the stations arm would grab hold of the outside of SD's ship and then the emergency inflatable tube would be deployed.

And that's when thousands of years of history with electric charge bit them all… Ruby saw it all on the display screen, which was piping in a view that SD had of a camera on the outside of his ship.

One moment the arm was slowly heading towards the hull, then in the next moment, almost immediately before it made contact, Ruby saw the *ZAP!* of charge move from SD's ship to the arm, imparting a small force on the ship and causing all manner of commotion on the operations center of the station.

Ruby heard cursing over the open line and a jumble of people speaking over each other.

But Ruby knew what had happened, she had seen it. She thought through what she knew of ESD and what to do. She was trying to ignore all the beeps, chirps, and tones the robots were making so she could think.

"Milo," she said, "what's standard procedure on Astroll 2

in case of an ESD event?"

Milo's eyes went wide in understanding.

"Uh," he said, obviously trying to recall what he knew, "it's always about the ship, not the station. The station is a large ground. For a ship, we would… we evacuate the ship."

"But there's nothing wrong with this ship, is there SD?" Ruby asked.

SD stopped his beeps and chirps long enough to answer, "Correct. There was minor damage to the outer hull, but we are fine."

Professor Coronik moved close to the microphone and spoke, "Legacy Station. What is your status?" There was still the jumble of sounds. Ruby looked at the viewscreen and saw that a portion of the ring, starting where the arm was connected, seemed to be lacking power. She made that determination based on the lack of any lights and that the arm seemed to be moving listlessly.

"Something happened and we lost power to proton repellents and the plasma mirror," came a voice. "Standby as we restore. Please retreat to 500 meters."

SD looked at Ruby, who nodded in agreement that this sounded like the right thing to do.

"I don't understand," Milo said, "why this didn't happen when our mini-R-pods, either yours or mine, docked with this ship?"

Ruby felt the inside of the wall and thought about it. It was cool, but not like the coated metallic alloy that was typical of their ships and Astroll 2. It almost had a feel of plastic to it, but not quite plastic.

"It must be this material that the inside of their ships is constructed with or lined with. It must be deliberately electrically dissipative," she said.

Milo touched it as well. And so did Disto.

"Do you have tactile sensors?" Disto asked.

"Yes," said Ruby. "But they're limited. Do you understand what just happened?"

Disto put an appendage on the wall to mirror Ruby's. He

shook his chassis to indicate he had no clue.

"We caused an electrical surge that may have damaged the station," Ruby said, and from the color that both Disto and SD turned, she felt bad for saying it that way.

"It's not your fault," Ruby said. "None of us thought of it. One of us probably should have. We're just uh, not used to alien vessels and might need to rethink some of our procedures if we're going to do this again."

"I wonder if AT could have helped fix it," SD said. Ruby put her hand that was not attached to the wall softly on the pocket that she carried AT in. He likely would have jumped at the chance, even the remote possibility of being useful. It was not lost on Ruby that at every opportunity, AT had offered to help—to help fix something, learn something, repair something. His base programming *needed* to be utilized. If he was human, with human emotions, she would say he was frequently some combination of bored, agitated, and anxious. She still didn't know what the robot equivalent was.

Ruby took her hand off the wall. Milo had already done so and was back looking at the viewscreen, his arms crossed in front of his chest as he concentrated.

"The damage doesn't look that bad," he said. "They probably need to replace the Cermg fuses that are super common and they're certainly going to have tons of spares. Maybe even their proton repeller, but that's not something that will prevent us from docking again. I'm sure they have a spare for that, too."

"I feel bad that we didn't think of this before," Ruby said.

"Yeah, me too," said Milo. "But this just doesn't happen. Our stuff is built with all this cemented in mind. *No one* thinks about it anymore."

Ruby shrugged.

"Hey," Milo said, putting a hand on her shoulder. "Don't beat yourself up about it, okay? Like I said, it doesn't look that bad. One thing at a time."

It felt like a million things at a time. But she took a deep breath and got ready for the *next* thing.

Chapter 26

> Ruby <

"It was Jade's idea to put your grandmother in this facility. At the time, your mom had connections to the University that manages it. The White-David Focality for Geriatrics is the most advanced facility anywhere in North America with respect to aging and elder care. Your grandmother was not quite old enough, officially… but, well, Jade took care of that."

Ruby gave her uncle a sidelong glance. She had learned more about her mother in the last 24 hours than she had in… years.

Now, Uncle Blake was telling her that her mother hacked systems to get what she wanted or needed.

Uncle Blake must have seen the look on her face. He smiled.

"It's not as bad as it sounds," he said, smiling. "Your grandmother's official records already didn't reflect her correct age. She had paid someone years earlier to make her 15 years younger than she was."

"Seriously?"

"To prevent someone from doing what your mother did. We think she was starting to recognize that she needed help. To your grandma's credit, she resisted and survived as long as possible."

Ruby looked out the window of the transport. It was a

private air transport that Coronik secured for them. Everything inside it was plush, and the pleasant scent of orange mixed with cardamom was deliberately piped into the air circulation system. The entire interior was designed for comfort and to keep its occupants relaxed, but Ruby couldn't do that.

She was thinking about Disto and the others and hoped they were okay. She was certain they were. It was generally known that they had come down to Earth via the space elevator which put them on a man-made island in the middle of the Pacific Ocean. From there, Coronik had flown all of them on their first private air transport to the mainland of the United States. To Omaha, Nebraska—site of the Church's North American Headquarters. Coronik mentioned that they should continue on to Scotland, but a conversation between him and Blake kept them in North America.

Blake had secured this side trip, while Disto and SD would remain with Coronik for now. Disto was going to get to his DNA tests. But SD? She wasn't sure exactly what they were doing with SD, but Coronik had promised that both robots would be well cared for, and just as importantly, he had the resources to keep their location a secret. Coronik also was able to provide Disto with a modified communicuff he could wear around his primary appendage. It wasn't as useful as her own, since communicuffs were designed to work with a biological user, but they'd at least be able to call each other. Ruby was thankful for that.

With the comfort of being able to contact her alien friends, Ruby's mind shifted to her grandmother.

"Remind me why we're going?" Ruby said.

Blake ran his fingers through his hair. "You need a connection to Earth. More than me and Logan have been able to provide. I know you think Astroll 2 is your home. It's not. It's just a place we've been living for a while. I know that 'while' has been most of your life, and I'm sorry we didn't recognize it as it was happening. We should have brought you back here more often."

"Why didn't you?" Ruby didn't mean for this to come out

with attitude but couldn't help that it had.

Blake sighed. "We meant to. We always said we would, but as you know, trips between the station and Earth can be a hassle. The years passed, and it… We just didn't realize that we needed to."

They sat silently for most of the rest of the ride. Ruby leaned her head on Blake's shoulder and closed her eyes. She was feeling the weariness of prolonged travel. She opened them when she felt the plunk of the transport stop, and the metallic sound of an artificial voice over the speaker said, "Arrival at Zappa Memorial Airport. Current time, 10:32am. Current temperature 88 degrees. Please ensure you remove any belongings."

A hatch opened slowly, and Ruby felt a kind of air that was strange to her. It was astonishingly moist. Even at the space elevator landing, she had been in enclosed spaces the whole time. This was the first time she was truly outside. Intellectually, she knew the difference between 'fresh' air and the recycled air she breathed. Intellectually, she understood it was summertime, and much of the Northern Hemisphere on Earth was hot, and often humid. But feeling it was not the same as knowing.

Knowing felt like she was submerged in a certain level of chaos. Suddenly, she found herself wondering if she was going to want to wear shorter pants for the summer heat, and she became worried about mosquitos. She'd only heard of them but associated them with summertime and didn't want to find herself itchy, or too hot, or any other number of variable concerns that Earth brought to her mind. She couldn't imagine being in a jungle, a forest, or even an open field.

She got up and looked out over the lot and to the awaiting car. It also bore the symbol of the Church, which is how she knew it was waiting for them.

"Do you need help?" Blake asked, watching her footsteps.

"No, I'm fine. A month at Location Zero did some good, I think." She stepped out of the pod and onto the lot and looked back at Blake. Eyebrows raised, she said, "Impressed?"

Blake laughed, "To be fair, you sort of cheated…"

Ruby scoffed, "And what about you? You and all your exercise?" Blake was holding on tight, and looked like he was moving through molasses.

"I'll be fine," he said. "Just need to move a little more."

They had both taken supplements meant to help people who were headed back to the gravity of Earth after a long time away. Usually, people took those supplements over several days on the trip back. But yesterday morning, they had woken up on Astroll 2. The trip was quicker than expected, so their bodies hadn't had time to let the supplements do their thing.

Once in the car, the automated voice said, "Please ensure your seatbelts are secure. We will commence movement in ten seconds. We will be at your destination in eight minutes."

The car was pre-programmed with the address of the facility.

Ruby had another eight minutes to think, and her brain didn't know where to begin. Should she think about her grandmother or look out the window at all the Earthly things there were to see? Out the window, nothing looked abnormal. While her memories of being here were fuzzy, she saw snippets of Earth all the time on vids. So, her brain decided to think about her grandmother instead. Would her grandmother even know it was her? She was certain probably not.

Once the car was at the facility, it said something about getting out, which they did. Blake led the way into the building. Ruby could see that the molasses effect was wearing off, and he was moving more like himself. She followed him, still feeling like she was carrying along a bag of rocks but also getting better with each movement as the seconds ticked by.

Two large doors swooshed open automatically as they approached, and Ruby followed Blake inside. Besides a few chairs, presumably for waiting, the lobby of the facility contained a floor-to-ceiling monitor inset into one wall that cycled through still images of smiling people, none of whom could have been less than 70 years old. Next to the monitor was a back-lit sign that read, "Welcome to the White-David

Focality for Geriatrics." At the far end of the lobby was a reception desk. Ruby observed the lack of a human receptionist. Instead, there was an artificial head at the end of a robotic arm. It detected their approach and said, "Welcome to the White-David Focality for Geriatrics. How may I help you?"

"We're here to see a resident. Name, Pearl Palmer."

"Please present identification so I may determine if you're on the approved visitors list."

Both Blake and Ruby spoke into their communicuffs, and holoimages appeared with their respective identification screens.

The robotic receptionist scanned them. First Blake, and it said out loud, "Blake Griffin. Approved to visit Pearl Palmer."

Next was Ruby. She held her arm up and the image faced the robot. The robot scanned it and said, "Ruby Palmer." Ruby would have sworn there was an extra half-second pause before it continued with, "Approved to visit Pearl Palmer."

"The resident is located in the FZC—the FunZone Common area—at this time. The lights will illuminate on the floor and wall of the corridor to show you the way."

"Thank you," Blake said and started to make his way to a corridor behind the reception desk. It wasn't lost on Ruby that he knew the procedure and where he was going. Even though it had to have been years since he'd been here himself.

"Wait," the robotic receptionist said.

They both turned back.

"Ruby Palmer. Ruby of the Robots?" it sounded like it was asking a question.

Ruby looked at Blake. "Uh, I guess?" she said.

"Thank you for bringing them here."

"Uh, okay," she said, again looking at Blake, whose eyebrows were drawn together. He didn't say anything but continued to walk through the door that swooshed open and into a corridor. Ruby followed.

"That was weird," Ruby said.

"Agreed," Blake responded. Then he shook his head in a

way that brought him back to the here and now. "Here. Your grandmother is down this residence hallway to the right."

The residence hallway emptied into an open common area with lots of windows and greenery both inside and out.

Several people, obviously residents, were intermixed with a few people who were obviously not residents. Assorted robots that were essentially mobile arms were also peppered in amongst the humans. Ruby saw one giving a metal cup of something to a resident. Medicine perhaps. Another was taking away a tray of what she hoped was uneaten mashed potatoes. And yet another was performing what might have been a form of physical therapy.

At a table, under a beautiful potted tree, sat a woman who looked eerily familiar. As if Ruby was looking into a mirror of herself aged up sixty or so years.

The table contained a game. It looked like chess, but the playing field was round. On the other side of the table, was another one of those robot arms.

"Check mate!" shouted the woman and stood up, spying Ruby and Blake out of the side of her eye, "and just in time, too. I have visitors!"

This woman, completely mobile, approached them.

"Blake!" she hugged him, then held him back so she could study him, then kissed one side of his face then the other.

"And this one. The offspring of my beloved Jade," and she embraced Ruby in a bearhug that belied her age again.

"Ruby," Ruby said.

"Oh, I know exactly who you are!" Pearl Palmer said, breaking the hug but still holding on to Ruby's upper arms. "Just let me look at you for a moment." And she did, her eyes going up and down Ruby, as if she was examining every cell.

"These clothes are so bland, darling," she said. "Come," and she grabbed Ruby's hand. "I have something for you."

Ruby had no choice but to follow where her grandmother led. The grip was strong. Blake followed too, and Ruby looked behind and mouthed "my clothes?" and then turned back to study this oddly strong woman who was wearing pajama pants and an open bathrobe that revealed a T-shirt with a faded symbol that she couldn't quite make out.

Pearl led Ruby and Blake back to a small room whose door had been left open. It was little more than a bed and a small kitchenette all in one. It was Pearl's room, as evidenced by the small LED screen next to the door that displayed "Pearl Palmer," each letter cycling through a rainbow of colors.

"Sit, let me find it..." She started opening and closing drawers, occasionally reaching her hand in to move the contents about.

Eventually, after about the seventh drawer, she said, "Ah!" and pulled out a chunky necklace.

"Here," she said to Ruby holding it out. "This is what you need. Some pop!"

Ruby took the offered gift and turned it around in her hand. It was lighter than it looked, probably some form of plastic made to look like stones. It was colorful, but in an earthy way.

"What is it?" she asked.

"It's a jade necklace. I always liked jade and other stones. That's why I named your mother Jade. Your mother, on the other hand, liked the sparkly stuff. Which is why she named you Ruby."

"How do you know that?" Ruby asked.

"Ha! I was there," Pearl Palmer looked at Blake. "How do I know? How can she ask that?" She pointed her thumb at Ruby in mock disgust. "Does she not know I was there?"

Blake looked at Ruby, his arms crossed, and he was leaning on a wall, clearly enjoying watching the interactions. "Your grandmother was there when you were born," he said matter-of-factly.

Ruby looked at the floor, trying to grasp an impossible memory, "I thought you were there, Uncle Blake?"

"I was. Too. We both were."

Ruby held the necklace in her hand and turned it over, "This isn't real jade. It's too light."

Her grandmother smiled, "Of course it isn't! Do you think I could afford such a thing! But does it matter? It looks like jade. That's what counts."

"Don't just stare at it," she continued. "Put it on!"

"Over this?" Ruby looked down at herself. She was still wearing the utility pants she put on before leaving Astroll 2 and a white, long-sleeve shirt with the station logo on it. She had her jacket on, too, which was the same color and material as her pants, with nearly as many pockets. She took it off, to reveal the full effect of the shirt.

The background of the logo was purple and had what were meant to be two brown asteroids, but that most people assumed were meatballs. Ruby tilted her head, "I don't think it's going to go..."

"Just humor an old lady, will you? You can take it off before you leave."

Ruby relented and unclasped the necklace, wrapped it around her neck, and let the clasp re-engage.

She put her jacket back on, which covered up the logo and looked at herself in the large mirror that was over the dresser in the room.

With the logo covered up, she admitted to herself that it didn't look terrible.

"See? Pop!" said Pearl, and she clapped her hands together to emphasize the 'pop!' "So, keep that. Keep some pop in your life, ok?"

Ruby nodded and smiled weakly in thanks, wondering if she could have predicted that this day would include acquiring a necklace that was clearly introduced to remind her of her mother.

Speaking of her mother, "Jade is what I wanted to talk about," Blake said next.

Blake sat down at one of the three chairs arranged around a small table that made up most of the kitchenette. He nodded at Ruby to take another.

Pearl sat in the plush chair by the window, crossing her feet under her as she did so. The light came in and was bright enough that it almost made Pearl look like she was glowing. All of her lines, the faint, violet lipstick, and the shimmering silver throughout her hair showed themselves better in the light. She seemed to be aware of this, as her back straightened and her demeaner seemed drawn to the window.

Ruby's assessment was that this woman, who was supposed to be in her 80s, was physically as spry as she had been in her 30s or 40s. Nothing about her seemed frail in the least. Ruby wondered what she would be doing if she wasn't here, and from her lucidity so far, wondered if it could be a mistake that she was here at all.

"Jade—*real* jade—absorbs your negative energy. I used to wear a jade bangle when I was young. Once I was in an accident, and the bangle broke. I walked away without a scratch!"

And maybe she does belong here after all, Ruby thought.

"Not your old jade jewelry," Blake continued, not asking any of the 100 questions that her snippet of a story begged. "I want to talk about Jade, your daughter."

"To outlive one's children is a curse of the gods!" she said, and her face took on a distant look. "It's my fault you know…"

"It's not," said Blake.

"It is! She didn't come to see me before like I had asked. I had an obsidian bracelet for her to take with her. If she had worn that! Its powers would have helped her…"

Yep, she belongs here.

Blake pulled up his chair until it was right in front of Pearl. "Jade died because of an accident. An accident during her operation. You are not responsible."

"Then who is?" she shot back a look. "My granddaughter lost her mother. Someone needs to be responsible for that."

Ruby was glad that Blake was here. She didn't know what to say to this woman, minute to minute. She was all over the place.

"We wanted to know what Jade told you about her work. I hadn't seen much of her in the year prior. We were just so busy… but I know she was here."

Ruby's grandmother looked back and forth between them.

"Do you want her journals?"

"Her, uh, journals?" Blake said.

"My mom kept a journal?" Ruby said.

"Oh yes. Since she was ten or so. I got her very first one for her. It was blue, with an image of a flower on top. I promised her she could write anything, and I would never read it."

Ruby stood up. "Do you mean like a real journal? With paper?"

"Yes, that's what I said."

Pearl untwisted herself from her plush chair and went over to the closet. She touched the side and the door slid open, accordion folding on itself. What was shown was a mess and Ruby's grandmother started removing stuff, placing things randomly on the table and the floor next to them.

"Blake, help move some of this, will ya? I'm old and frail!"

Ruby got the sense that she liked saying that as a form of irony. This woman was not frail.

After a few minutes, she declared "ah ha!" and pulled out a plastic box that emerged from the bottom of the closet, having been underneath a pile of stuff.

She sat on the floor with her legs wrapped around it and opened it.

She frowned, "This isn't it. Darling, you'll have to come back. Maybe it's in my storage facility…" she mumbled some more that Ruby couldn't hear.

"I think it's time for us to go," Blake announced quite abruptly.

"But Jade needs to take her journals back," Ruby's grandmother stood up and had the look of a toddler who just asked for a favorite toy. "Don't you want to keep up your journal writing my lovely, Jade? Now that you're back from your secret assignment?"

Ruby looked at Blake whose eyes had sunken in. He also recognized that Pearl was losing her hold on any lucidity she had projected only a few moments ago.

Ruby's grandmother hugged her and went back to her plush chair. But instead of crossing her legs underneath her like she had before, now she sat like an old woman. Feet on the ground, hands in her lap, she stared out of the window.

Did she realize the mistake she had just made?

After a moment, she looked at Blake. Even though she was looking at him, it somehow seemed like she was looking past him. She said, "I hope they'll turn on the news after dinner again. My granddaughter has been on the news. Do you know her? Ruby Palmer. She's famous! First human to meet an alien! Isn't that amazing? I hope she'll come visit me…"

Ruby opened her mouth to remind her grandmother that she was right there, but Blake put a hand up to stop her and shook his head.

"I hope so, too, Ms. Palmer," he said and took a small fleece blanket that had been folded up at the foot of her bed and placed it on her lap. "I'll let them know they should turn on the news."

"Robots…" she said, talking to no one, but again looking out the window at the courtyard that was still getting some light from the now setting sun. "Robots from space. Who knew? My Jade knew… that's who." She was mumbling, almost incoherent, but Ruby swore that as Blake was ushering them out, she heard a final mumble, "…and that's why they had her killed."

Once they were outside the room, the door swished shut behind them.

"What the… what the was that?" Ruby didn't know what to say.

"She has psychotic episodes. You know that's why she's here," Blake said calmly.

As if on cue, a robotic arm following a line on the floor rolled up to the room and pushed the intercom. "Ms. Palmer, I'm here with your evening meds and tests." Ruby didn't see it push any button to open the door, but the door appeared pre-programmed to open after the robot announced itself. Once open, the robotic arm continued to follow the lines inside. The door stayed open, and Ruby heard her grandmother say "Oh, thank you dear!" followed by a robotic "Please extend your arm."

Blake peeked in, but then said, "We should go."

As they were walking out, they passed more of these arms. Several were headed into the residential rooms. It must be med time, Ruby thought.

They were back in the reception lobby. "Can you call the car service?" Blake asked.

Ruby spoke into her communicuff, and Pippa acknowledged the request.

"Two minutes," she said.

The large monitor was still cycling through images of smiling people and now there was a robot arm with the human every third or fourth image or so. She was certain there were no robots in the images when they came through earlier. She was also certain that the artificial head at the end of the receptionist arm was smiling in her direction.

"And I think I'm going to spend the rest of these two minutes waiting outside," she said to Blake.

Chapter 27

> Detailed Historian <

Disto was a robot of many expectations. His expectation-generator algorithm had been working in overtime.

For one, Disto wasn't expecting to be the only robot in the lab. He was hoping that SD would stay with him. Next, he was not expecting one of the human-created robots to assist him. He was expecting humans. And lastly, he expected to have some time between activities to watch more of the vids that he and SD had been enjoying, watching humans romp around and do everything imaginable. This expectation still had some hope of playing out.

It had been an interesting ride getting to this point. After coming down the space elevator from Legacy Station, they were all taken to a nondescript building that Professor Coronik called 'headquarters.' Once there, they all split up. Uncle Blake and Ruby were headed to visit another of Ruby's relatives. Milo had obligations to his employer. Disto had wanted SD to stay with him, but before he could protest, SD was whisked away with promises that he would be well cared for and excuses like how there wouldn't be enough room where Disto wanted to be.

'Headquarters' was in a location that the humans referred to as Omaha. Although Disto overheard Professor Coronik mutter, "The real headquarters is in Edinburgh. This is a local and poor substitute."

They were on the 10th level of a building that looked out along the rest of the city. Never had Disto predicted that he'd be standing on an alien world. He'd seen aliens, sure, but always on his own planet.

He wondered now how similar this world was to the other alien's homeworlds, such as the Clasuoids. Did they build structures into the sky from the surface of their world as well? Was the sky they looked up at even the same shade as the one on this world?

Disto's programming, to be concerned with his own history and the history of his planet didn't leave much room for thinking about other beings more than what was necessary to interact with them.

They weren't at 'Headquarters' long before he was whisked away to another building. He was told he would be in the same city, although he had no way to verify this. The location markers he relied upon on Location Zero didn't exist here. The walls of Location Zero were always marked so he could precisely locate his position.

Here, in every structure he'd seen on Earth so far, the walls were bare, at least with respect to the kind of positioning information that would be useful to him. Even upon initial entry to this most recent building. Professor Coronik did not bring him here. Instead, another human who bore some similarity to Milo, appeared.

"Xander Xander will take you to the laboratory. It's on the other side of the city, also in a building managed by the Church," Professor Coronik said by way of introduction.

Xander Xander held out his quivering hand. "I'm Professor Coronik's assistant," he said with a half grin. "I'm being temporarily reassigned to assist you." Disto observed that Xander Xander looked for confirmation from Coronik, who nodded calmly.

Xander Xander held a tablet close to his chest and walked around Disto. Disto turned a little in one direction and then quickly turned in the other direction to meet Xander Xander's gaze when he was nearly complete with his circumnavigation of Disto.

"Do you approve?" Disto asked.

"Su-sure?"

"I have been studying the reactions of humans ever since I met Ruby. I interpret your... body language... as nervousness? Am I making you nervous?" Disto asked. "That is not my intent."

Xander Xander straightened up, and a small smile appeared on the lower portion of his face.

"Ok. It's okay. Let's get going, shall we?"

From then to now, in the lobby of this other nondescript building, whatever Xander Xander had experienced was gone and an air of confidence had replaced it.

In the lobby of the new building, Xander Xander said, "Wait here," and he approached another human behind a counter.

While waiting, there were a handful of other humans who had probably been intending to pass through the lobby, but who slowed down or stopped completely to look at Disto.

Disto remembered that he was fully briefed on the fact that this was the first contact with beings from outside their solar system, so the robots would experience anything and everything from mild curiosity to fear and rage. Humans had a wide range of emotions. Predicting them without knowing the specific individual ahead of time was nearly impossible. Disto was beginning to notice that each human had their own way of showing different emotions. Ruby paced when she was trying to solve a problem, but her Uncle Blake crossed his arms. It was disorienting to find the nuances between the extraordinary number of variables. To Disto, it seemed an impossible feat for any human to understand anyone else at all. Or even themselves for that matter.

The group of humans starting to surround Disto seemed the curious type. Curiosity was something that Disto understood intrinsically, probably because it was part of his own programming. Curiosity was a key component in ensuring that he was able to carry out his mission.

There was a low level of conversation happening around him that he wasn't a part of.

He listened in where he could. Two humans—it took him a few moments to match sound to bodies—were discussing his construction.

"The mobility is very reminiscent of mid-21st century robots," one said.

"They must not have steps."

"Yeah, you heard, it was a whole planet of them… a whole planet on the surface?"

Disto, if he was programmed to chuckle, would at the misinformation regarding his planet. Ruby's description must not have made it out for the rest of the humans to consume. They were speculating on some of the basic facts about his planet and getting them wrong.

He would have corrected them himself, but Xander Xander was back at his side saying, "Follow me!"

The sea of onlookers parted and Xander Xander escorted him through what he described as a 'security checkpoint' and then to a lift. It was amusing that humans had lifts that were nearly identical to the ones on Location Zero. Surprising especially to Disto, because human's locomotive appendages were so different from the robots of Location Zero. He wondered how two historically different origins could reach the same end point.

The lift was empty except for the two of them. "We'll be on the 14th floor," Xander Xander said. "Once you're situated, I need to run an errand. Let me know if you need anything before I go."

Disto thought about whether he should make Xander Xander aware of his power situation, which continued to concern him. He was good for the moment, but sometimes there were glitches. Luckily, AT had Disto store an extra power cell before they left Location Zero and the moment they arrived at Astroll 2, AT figured out how to connect him into the human's power system.

Disto wondered how robots on this planet were powered and if they could experience similar disturbances.

"Are there humans who are experts on human-developed robots?" he decided to ask.

"Yes," Xander Xander said as the lift came to a stop and the door opened. He pointed out into the hallway, indicating that Disto should go first, then Xander Xander came out and started in a direction. Disto wondered how he knew where to go but followed all the same.

"I would like to talk to one," Disto said.

"Well, I uh, know a little about robotics," he said.

Xander Xander didn't look like someone who knew about robotics. He wasn't sure what a human who did was supposed to look like, but Xander Xander clearly didn't fit that image that Disto clearly didn't have. Clearly.

Disto must have been taking too long to process that information, so Xander Xander added. "It's my parents. They owned a company that manufactured robot arms. It didn't do well—they were great engineers but terrible businesspeople. I was working in the factory when it was bought up by the Church, and long story short, my skills were better suited to what I do now."

"You are an assistant?"

"Correct."

"What is that?"

"Well, I do whatever is needed. One day that might be making travel arrangements for Professor Coronik to visit Astroll 2. Another day that might be escorting an alien robot to a lab to do… what exactly?"

Disto re-explained the whole story of the lost data he was hoping to find in the junk DNA of Earth's biological creatures.

"Then why are you looking for a roboticist?"

"It's a," Disto ensured he chose the right word, "personal problem."

Xander Xander looked Disto up and down and Disto wondered if Xander Xander possessed special optical sensors that could diagnose his problem right then. Afterall, his face held some object that he had seen on a few humans. This one was rimmed bright blue. But he had already seen Xander Xander remove the device several times.

"Is that a diagnostic tool?"

"Oh this? These are my glasses. I had my eyes done years ago, but I still like the look. Someone told me I looked good in them once and it kinda stuck."

"So, not a diagnostic tool?"

"No. Purely for decoration. If they're distracting, I can put them away?"

"No," Disto said.

They had now been outside a room for a few moments. While they were talking Disto watched Xander Xander press a pad on the side of the door more than once and looked at his tablet and poked at it. It was fascinating that humans had the ability to interleave their actions to create the appearance that they were doing more than one thing at a time. What had Ruby called it? "Multi-tasking?"

"Although everyone knows it's not real multi-tasking. It's an illusion," she had said. "And I try not to do it. Very inefficient."

Apparently, not all humans shared the same—Disto was trying to remember the concept and word—opinion, yes, the same opinion as Ruby on the topic since this human was interleaving like his life depended on it.

Finally, the door swooshed open.

"Finally!" Xander Xander said.

He walked in and was greeted by another human. Disto looked around the room. It was lined with tables and computer consoles and approximately every other table included a clear box with equipment either poking out of it, poking into it, or stationed next to it.

"Welcome to the Church's Deep Bio Lab," the new human said. "I am Dr. Cairo Coates." She held out a hand, and Xander Xander made contact with his own hand. Disto's appendages were all stowed, and before he had a chance to extend one, Dr. Coates had returned hers to its default position along her side.

The two humans moved to the other side of the room. While Xander Xander didn't say it aloud, Disto felt there was an implied 'stay here,' and he did, taking in the sights of the room.

Upon his second scan, he realized the room was three or four times his original impression. One of the walls wasn't a wall at all, but a set of shelves. There was room to move on either side, and once someone was beyond that fake wall, Disto could see the room continue. That section of the room was somewhat different from this. The lighting was still the same, but there were a handful of robotic arms that moved around on the floor. They moved slowly, slower than was his typical speed, but once they stopped that locomotion, their upper arm movements started and those were fast. Potentially faster than he was capable of moving his own appendages.

He started moving in that direction until he heard, "Disto, not yet! There's a safety video you need to watch first!"

It was Xander Xander calling after him. Xander Xander and Dr. Cairo Coates apparently had finished their chat.

"And we need to sanitize you and figure out how you're going to wear typical lab gear," said Dr. Coates.

Disto had no idea what that last utterance meant but was inclined to let them do what they needed to do. He was happy to watch a video and comply with actions that needed to be done.

He was so close to potentially finding his data!

"And I'm going to need someone to educate me on how to perform a DNA test."

Both Xander Xander and Dr. Cairo Coates looked at each other. "You don't know how to do this?"

"I'm a historian, not a biologist."

Both humans simultaneously replicated a motion that Ruby made all the time. They put their palms to their face and said what sounded like, "Ugh."

> Swell Driver <

Swell Driver didn't want to leave Disto. He was looking forward to helping, but two humans told him he needed to follow them. He briefly considered protesting but could not compute a positive outcome to that action, so did as he was instructed.

Along the way, he wished he had ignored that computational result and protested anyway, but now it was too late. He was far out of range to communicate with Disto. He did not know where Ruby was, either. He wished he had simply stayed on his ship.

The two humans he followed were covered in identical clothing. The growth on their heads was also identically colored and identically shaped. He was only able to discriminate between the two because one was slightly taller than he was, and the other seemed to be of an average height for a human.

He was also able to differentiate because one walked behind him and the other stayed in front—the one he was instructed to follow.

SD was not really paying attention to the surroundings they walked him through other than to memorize the directionality. He could turn around and return to the spot where he left Disto at any moment.

But he didn't. Instead, he followed these humans until they brought him into a large room.

"Wait here," they said.

Before they could shut the door behind him, SD called out, "Wait! Can I watch… vids?"

One of the humans re-entered the room, touched a panel on one of the walls, and it came to life. "Do you know how to use the selector?" he asked.

SD didn't, so the human proceeded to explain what to do to access a large compendium of human-made vids and how to search for and play any individual vid. SD scrolled through the list in awe, not noticing when the humans finally left him alone.

SD first searched his own recent memory to see if any of the vids in the available index matched a title that Ruby had mentioned. He'd want to watch those first. "I love all the old movies that had to do with space travel," she had said. "Oh, and time travel, too. Especially ones that combined those."

SD used the search feature and found movies that met those criteria, beginning with ones humans created nearly 200 years earlier.

He could control the rate that the vids played, and by the time one of the two humans returned, while it had only been a few thousand clicks, SD had managed to watch a large quantity of vids. He was re-watching one where humans—with FTL capability—traveled to their past, rescued additional biological creatures, and returned to the future.

"…*pick up enough speed, you're in time travel, if you don't, you're fried…*" came the words from the vid right before the human shut it off.

SD was about to protest and then realized it wasn't the same human that brought him to this room but Professor Coronik.

"Tell us about your ship, SD," he said. "We'd like to know all about it."

"Who is 'us' and 'we'?" SD asked. Professor Coronik was the only human in the room with him.

Coronik tapped his fingers a few times on the wall panel once more, and again the screen came alive. This time, instead of a vid, it was a face. Not quite a human face, but not as simple as his facial representation on his own face-screen. Something in between these two.

"Swell Driver, meet TERP," Coronik said. "TERP, and I, want to learn everything about your ship. And you."

Chapter 28

> Detailed Historian <

To both Xander Xander and Dr. Coates' surprise, Disto was a quick study. He only needed to receive the instructions once. In this case, he wasn't really testing any actual DNA. He was referring to a computer that had the DNA mapped. He was scanning DNA.

"We could have sent you this data," Dr. Coates said. "You didn't need to come all this way."

In fact, Disto could have done this from anywhere. He was looking at DNA for the sequences that humans referred to as 'junk,' and if the DNA was already mapped, all the better.

The task at hand was searching as efficiently as possible through the data to find a certain marker.

Disto was lost in his circuits and didn't notice that the communicuff he had been given was making noise.

"Someone is calling you," Dr. Coates called out from across the room. She was still there, carrying on with her own work after having mentioned that she couldn't leave an alien robot alone in her laboratory when Disto suggested that she didn't need to stay on his account.

Disto then heard Dr. Coates, who had been as gracious as was possible for any human, mutter under her breath about wishing she had the opportunity to just send the data instead of playing host and babysitter.

As a Historian, Disto came preprogrammed with a search algorithm that he could use to help with historical research.

He set his algorithm to find the certain piece of DNA, and it was already working when he answered his communicuff. It was Ruby.

"I just wanted to check in," she said. Her face was visible on a holoscreen above the table that Disto had set the communicuff down upon.

"Apparently, all the data existed. I'm solely engaged in a search process."

"Really? What kind of search algorithm are you using?"

"There are different types? I only contain one such algorithm."

"Uh oh…" Ruby said.

"What's wrong?"

"I'm going to make an educated guess about your search algorithm. It's linear."

Disto took a look at a copy of it while the primary one continued its execution.

"I am not sure what you mean by 'linear.' It systematically examines each item for the search criteria. If the search criteria are not detected, it moves on to the next item," Disto said.

"Yup. Linear. Ugh. Disto… you're going to be there all month."

"That could present a problem." Disto had expected he would be done in a day. Maybe two days.

"Yes, a big problem," Ruby agreed. "And I'm going to guess that you have no other algorithms at your disposal for this?"

"Why would someone need more than one?"

"For the reason I just said," Ruby said, "or, rather, I implied. Efficiency. Speed."

Ruby went on to explain, "How many comparisons can you do in one tic?"

Disto examined the data so far and responded, "Ten, on average."

"And if you have a million of these comparisons to do, how

long is it going to take?"

Disto did the math, including converting it into Ruby's time system, which was the local time system. "More than a day," he said.

"And how many millions of these do you need to do?"

Disto wasn't exactly sure. Each DNA sequence of each biological organism had a long strand of junk DNA, and he was looking for a short sequence of that to be the marker. But he recognized the point that Ruby was trying to make.

"How do I speed up this process?" he asked.

"I'm so glad you asked," Ruby said. "Give me a few minutes, and I'll figure out which is the best. I'm thinking not a binary search or anything else that requires a sorted array to work well... linear search is usually the way to go, but there's got to be some ways to make it more efficient. You keep it going, let me call you back in a few, okay?"

Ruby's face disappeared.

Disto considered what she had said about making his algorithm more efficient. He was no Algorithm Pioneer, but was he capable of figuring out on his own how to make it go faster?

Right now, the process involved letting the data pass through his circuits. Then one of his processors executed the algorithm. But this room was full of computers, and to his understanding, each computer had one or more processors. He wondered if they were inherently faster or slower.

"Could I access one of your computers to aid in my search?" Disto asked Dr. Coates. She didn't hear him, so she didn't answer, and Disto really didn't want to bother her anymore. He was already plugged into one of the computers. That's how he was being fed data.

Without disturbing the in-process search, Disto pinged the processor only to find out that it indeed performed more calculations in a tic, or rather, in a second. He had to start thinking in human-based timescales while he was here on their planet, using their equipment.

This computer contained multiple processors. He activated

his search in one of them and measured the results. It made four times as many comparisons in a second.

Excellent! I can already speed up my search by a factor of four.

Disto was so proud of himself and wanted to call Ruby back. *But could I do even better?*

Disto did something rare for a Historian. He looked at the search algorithm to see how it worked. Disto was not the kind of robot that went around looking and examining algorithms. There were other robots for that, and it felt wrong to do so. But those robots were not available, and he had good reason to support his actions. He was trying to make it better, on behalf of the Special Project, and didn't that make it ok?

As he examined the algorithm, he saw that it treated the input data as an array and started at the beginning, going one by one, element by element as it made the comparison.

What if it started both at the beginning and the end, he thought? Then it could make a second comparison at the same time. If nothing was found for a given array, in theory, it should have taken half the time.

Disto made the changes and then set it to work on yet another processor in the computer and proved that yes, it did speed up the process by another factor of two.

During this, he realized that if he were to let this computer do it, with its 16 processors… well, that's another factor of 16!

This would be done in no time.

Over the next few minutes, and with Dr. Coates' help, he did just that. He made full use of the computer, with his algorithm running in each of the 16 processors.

"Are you sure this isn't a bother?" Disto asked Dr. Coates.

"This is one of our older computers. No one usually uses it."

Disto was pleased that he wasn't interrupting anyone else's work. While he felt that his work was of the utmost importance, he could recognize that to another individual, whether robot or human, they would view their work as the utmost importance from their perspective and he didn't want to get in the way of that.

"In fact," Dr. Coates added, "you don't have to stay here. The computer, while old, is still on the network and we can set it up so that it will send you results periodically or when it's done."

"Ooo periodically, if that's possible!" Disto was excited.

Dr. Coates smiled. Disto wished he knew if that smile was that she was happy to be helping Disto or happy that she found a way for this alien to not be around. Disto was aware that not all humans wanted to be around him and his robot kind but was having difficulty predicting or determining which way any particular human preferred.

But Dr. Coates continued to help, and they tested to ensure that Disto could receive a notification on his version of the communicuff.

Disto called Ruby back.

"I did it!" Disto said proudly.

"You did what? You found what you were looking for?"

"No, I sped up the algorithm by four, and then by two, and then by 16!"

Ruby's eyes went wide in the hologram and Disto went on to explain exactly what he did and how and that he could let it run.

"It will still take a day or more to complete the search," he said.

"Well, ok! Let's arrange to get you out of there and meet back up."

Disto called back Xander Xander who was pleased that Disto was ready to depart, saying, "TERP wants to see you. He has, a, uh, *test* in mind." Once more, Disto repeated his story of triumph with the search algorithm to Xander Xander, all the while wondering if triumphant would be an accurate representation if the algorithms didn't return a positive match. For the moment, he'd accept the small success, but as the time went on, he was growing less optimistic that a positive match would be the case. This, he kept to himself.

There were still more than seven hundred thousand DNA samples to test. This planet had a lot of biological life.

"That's great," Xander Xander said. "But we have to get you over to the quiz show where TERP wants to play."

"Play?" Disto asked.

Chapter 29

> Ruby <

"This can't be right," Ruby said, looking out the window of the DAVe. This particular DAVe—Dynamic Autonomous Vehicle—was particularly cozy and something Ruby and her family would normally not be able to afford. It was a gift from AATR, the company that made them. She tried to refuse, but they also offered to make sure that the vehicle could be housed and maintained if she went back to Astroll 2—as long as they could use her likeness in advertising materials. She had little interest in automobiles—spaceships were more her thing—but the convenience was not easy to pass up.

"Pippa, repeat Disto's message."

"It was," Pippa began, "'Ruby, there is no information in this DNA. The humans I am with said you should meet us at the address I am about to transmit.'" Pippa paused and then said, "And before you ask for a fourth time, yes, I have voice analyzed that message. Analysis confirms it is Disto with a 99.97% certainty factor."

The address that Disto passed along was a street that had not been maintained to the standards that DAVes typically drove on. There was too much gravel, broken glass that glittered in the Sun, and other pulverized road schmutz that hadn't yet made it off to the sides of the road.

Uncle Blake sat next to her and looked out the other

window. "Let's keep going down the road a little more. Slowly."

"Of course, mate!" responded DAVe in an old-fashioned Australian accent. When the DAVe arrived to pick up Ruby and Blake, it asked for speech preferences, and Ruby simply responded, "Default," while she was fighting with the seatbelt strap that seemed already locked in place. 'Default' turned out to be a version of Australian she had only ever heard in movies.

As they creeped along the road, Blake and Ruby each continued to look out of their respective windows. There were buildings on each side, separated by alleyways that could fit maybe one singular narrow-modeled DAVe. The buildings themselves looked like they were probably warehouses or storage facilities. Maybe some were dated art studios. Most had that old look with an old-style roll-up garage door that would let in light, fresh air and that one little bug that would stick to wet paint and make the most pleasant artist curse the world like an angry God unleashing his wrath from the heavens.

The place seemed oddly devoid of any signs of human activity. Or any activity at all, for that matter. Ruby half-expected to see a feral cat or two. Or maybe a rogue mouse. But there was nothing.

Until nothing became something.

"Uncle Blake, I see people!" Ruby declared and pointed through the front window.

Indeed, they were now able to see a line of people snaking around from one of the alleyways. They continued to crawl forward, for there had been no command for DAVe to cease its forward motion, nor was anything truly in its way, since the line of people kept to the side of the building and out of the road.

As they got closer, Ruby could make out more details and swallowed hard. She again recognized some of the t-shirts a handful of these people were wearing.

Please let this fad pass quicker! Ruby silently prayed.

"Stop," Uncle Blake said. DAVe complied.

"What are you doing?" Ruby asked as Blake went for the

door handle.

"Going to go ask what's going on. I think this is probably what that address meant. Seems like we're supposed to be here, don't you think?"

Ruby knew that this made the most sense but didn't like the idea of letting any crowd of people see her. She wished she had grabbed a scarf or something from her grandmother. And sunglasses. And a blonde, bluntly banged wig.

She overheard Blake call out to one of the people in line. "What's this?"

"Line starts back there, buddy. You'll have to wait to get in like the rest of us." A bald man pointed his thumb that-a-way.

"Get into what?"

A small woman wearing a Pro-Ruby shirt gave the bald man a whack on the arm and said, "Steve, that was rude," and then to Blake, "This is where they tape NYAQS! They're doing a special show today. The notification that they were looking for audience members came in overnight. Usually, we have a week's notice or more."

Blake stuck his head back in so Ruby could see. "Sounds familiar, but as you know, I don't watch much. Do you know this NYAQS?"

"Uncle Blake, you know, except for old movies, I don't watch much either! Did you forget everything about me this last month?" Ruby teased and then got serious again. She sighed. "Pippa, what is NYAQS?"

Pippa responded immediately, "NYAQS, also known as 'Not Your Ancestors Quiz Show,' is a popular game show available to watch on most entertainment venues. It is derived from a 200-year-old game that implies it puts contestants in jeopardy, but instead of harming them, gave them money for answering questions correctly. Unlike its ancestor, when NYAQS first debuted, the producers had plans to cause injury to contestants who answered questions incorrectly, but quickly learned that was no incentive for being on the show and reverted to a format that was similar, but not entirely like the ancient show."

"Thank you, Pippa," Ruby said, remembering that Pippa liked to hear words of affirmation.

Blake was still standing outside the DAVe, leaning on the door, and looking around at the line of people. The line had grown slightly in the short time they were parked.

"Why would Disto tell us to meet him at a game show?" Ruby asked. She was asking Uncle Blake. Or Pippa. Or anyone who could answer. She'd even appreciate an answer from DAVe if it was programmed to give one.

"I think there's only one way we're going to find out," Blake responded.

"I was afraid of that," said Ruby. She looked around once more. "DAVe, you don't have an extra hat, do you?"

DAVe responded with a tone that sounded like a duck being squeezed.

"I guess not," Ruby said to herself.

She opened the door and stepped out. Blake had already closed his door and come around the car to her. She looked at the long line of people. No one seemed to notice. They were looking ahead in the line. Impatient and waiting for it to move. Most of them looked at some device or other. Many had the tinted sun-goggles that were currently in fashion, and most stared at some form of device on parts of their hands. Some had thumb rings, or communicuffs like hers.

This was all good news because no one had noticed her.

Until they did.

Within three seconds of hearing a voice call, "Oh my god! It's Ruby!" Everyone was looking at her. But they weren't swarming. Even though she heard her name over and over, with "I love you," and "come over here," and "is it true that the robots wouldn't let you brush your teeth," no one was willing to leave the line. They had to stay put, which only made them scream louder.

Ruby scanned the line up and down looking to see if she could make out Disto or SD. She wondered if they were even there.

She started making her way towards the front of her line,

making sure to keep more than an arm's length away from anyone. While they weren't leaving their place, they were reaching out and trying to touch her.

A pregnant woman was even shouting that Ruby needed to touch her belly. Something about making sure her baby was blessed. And then there were the picture requests. Ruby wasn't about to honor any of those right now. Luckily, Blake was there as a sort of bodyguard. He stayed in between the line of people and Ruby and also managed to stay out of arms reach.

As they approached the front, a woman, dressed in black pants and a black t-shirt, wearing blue tinted sun goggles came rushing toward them with her tablet in hand. Before Ruby could decide what this woman had the look of, she had stopped right in front of Ruby and Blake. Sweating, but not panting, she said, "Ruby Palmer. Excellent. We have a special seat reserved for you. Follow me."

The way this woman, who was nearly the exact same height as Ruby, looked nearly the exact same age, but sounded like she had twice as much going on in her life, said "Follow me," gave Ruby the impression that if any protest was attempted, the Universe would implode.

Ruby looked at Blake, who made the 'after you' gesture to follow the woman who had already begun to walk in the direction she came. It was also the direction toward the front of the line that they had already been walking, so presumably it was where they should have been heading anyway.

"I'm Rhon," the woman called back over her shoulder. She barely took the time to glance at them as she spoke. Her tablet kept buzzing, and she kept typing on it with her long, glass nails that matched the speed and clicking sound of her heels. "Short for Rhonda. Assistant producer. We're gathering you all in the green room…"

Ruby could barely hear over the on-going shouts of the people in line. When Rhon said the word 'room,' she simultaneously opened a door to the building that everyone was lined up to get into.

Ruby's eyes adjusted as they continued to follow Rhon

briskly past other people who were bustling about. These people also noticed Ruby, let their eyes go wide, but continued on with whatever task they were already engaged in.

The inside of this place matched the outside in a way that felt messy. The walls, ceiling, and even floor were painted a dark navy. Or maybe it was purple. It was too dark to tell, but whatever it was, it absorbed most of the light coming from the ceiling fixtures. The messiness feeling came from the clutter of stuff that was not really strewn about, but also not as neat as it could have been. A set of folded chairs was lined up along one wall, a few lying down for no obvious reason. Various sized shipping crates sat about with packing peanuts scattered around them on the floor. A rack of what looked like men's suits was pushed against one wall that looked like they were fresh off the runway of a fashion show.

Rhon stopped short and turned around, causing Ruby to nearly run into her, and Blake to nearly run into Ruby. Ruby couldn't see her eyes through the goggles but still could tell that Rhon was listening to something or someone. This was confirmed when she said, "Ok. Well, I have to bring her somewhere until… oh. There? That room isn't prepped. Well, someone better bring the food over… *yes* for the *robots*. Cheese quesadillas for the circuit boards! Just have it moved… right… exactly. Robots don't eat. Sarcasm. It was sarcasm, Carl. Get it done."

She let out an exasperated sigh.

"Ok, we're going to the Orange Room instead. Don't worry, there *will* be food for you if I have to move it over myself," she started moving a different way, and Ruby and Blake had no good choice but continue to follow her. "Fun fact! Assistant producers have to do *everything*. And don't even get me started on the lack of vacation time. You'd think a one week stay in the underwater city of Miami wouldn't be a big deal, but *no!*"

She opened a door and walked into a room that was, as promised, orange. Completely orange. Walls, ceiling, floor. And a faux fur area rug that took up most of the room that was also orange. A couch which lined one wall was a different shade of orange from the rest of the room, as were the three chairs. The only main component that was not orange was the oversized, neon-brown coffee table. In her short time back on Earth, Ruby instantly disliked the recent trend of neon brown because it was pretty much just orange with a trendier name, but no one seemed to acknowledge it. Entirely fitting for a place like this.

"The refreshments will be here in a minute, and I'll have my assistant over to prep you," she said as Ruby and Blake took spots on the couch. "I have 100 other things to do, and we go live in about 15 minutes."

Up until this point, Ruby hadn't said much. With the rush through the building and their busy tour guide slash assistant producer, she hadn't had a moment to ask a key question.

"Wait! Before you go," Ruby said, "What exactly are we going live for?"

Rhon was already rushing out of the room, and without eye contact or breaking stride simply responded, "Like I said, someone will come prep you."

"But—" Ruby called.

Rhon shut the door before any more questions could be asked.

Ruby sighed. "I've got a weird feeling about this."

Uncle Blake sat down on the fuzzy orange couch and reclined. "I don't think being broadcasted has ever given you a good feeling." He paused and then said, "For good reason."

Ruby frowned, "I just don't like leaving SD and Disto with other people for this long. I know they're looking for their data, and it's not like they belong to me, but… in a way, they're naive. I just—"

"You want to protect them."

"Yeah, exactly."

Uncle Blake winked. "They're not children. Which is a good thing, too. Children grow up and eventually steal spaceships, and…"

Ruby play-punched Blake's shoulder. "Too soon, Uncle

Blake. And it's not just that. I don't trust Coronik. And I know you don't, either. And that TERP system. The more I hear about it…" She trailed off.

"…the more you wonder if it's actually a computer virus?" Blake picked up where she left off.

"A virus? That can't be. A virus would be caught by protection software," Ruby said, remembering the recent experience she had with that and AT.

"Maybe not if it's a smart one. A smart and mutable one."

"Uncle Blake, you're scaring me," Ruby said. She meant it.

"Forget I said anything," he smiled. "Now where's that food we were promised? I'm a little hungry. Are you hungry?"

Ruby recognized Blake was trying to change the subject. And it was working. She was hungry.

Chapter 30

> Ruby <

No one came in those 15 minutes. The promised food never arrived either.

After about 16 minutes, Ruby said, "Should we go looking for someone?"

"I was thinking the same thing," Blake said.

"I'm hungry. And thirsty." Ruby thought fondly of the aforementioned cheese quesadillas. Her stomach grumbled. The mushed peas available in her grandmother's facility weren't appetizing, so it had been quite a while since Ruby had eaten.

The door opened, and Ruby's eyes were locked to find food. But it was just Rhon, with only her tablet in hand.

She clenched her jaw when she saw the empty coffee table, mumbled something that Ruby couldn't make out, and then said, "It's time. This way."

Ruby and Blake looked at each other.

"Time for what?" Blake said before Ruby could.

"Did Carl not prep you? Oh-em-gee-sticks! That's it, I don't care if he has his son's moonwalker training to pay off. I am firing him today. Right after this show. Which is starting, Ruby needs to take her place."

"My place?" Ruby said.

"Yes, there's a seat right in front of the stage where the

confidante is located."

"'Confidante?'" Uncle Blake questioned.

"Of course! You've seen the show before, right? It's the most popular game show on the planet. Everyone's seen it. Heck, they play it at daycare!"

"Um, well, I'd heard of it…" Ruby trailed off, not wanting to offend Rhon, but not wanting to lie, either.

Rhon closed her eyes, took a breath, and muttered, "Not prepped, empty stomachs, and they don't even know what-the-jam this show's about…" When she opened her eyes she said, "Just come with me. Both of you. We really don't have time."

Rhon walked ahead, but Ruby didn't follow. Instead, she said, "Look, I don't know if this is a good idea."

Rhon snapped her head back, gaze like a storm, but in a sing-songy, overly gentle voice, said, "You don't know if this is a good idea? Oh, Ruby Palmer, this is *not* the moment to do this to me."

Ruby shook her head, "Thank you for all the effort you've put in here, but I'm not going to wander onto a super popular show like a lost puppy dog. This whole thing… it's just not something I'm interested in."

Rhon, unphased, checked the time on her tablet. "Well, you should've thought about that before you decided to become a celebrity. I have a show to run."

Uncle Blake put up his hand and began to speak, but Ruby, face hot and fists clenched, got her words out first. "I. Didn't. Choose. This. I don't want any of this! I just want people to know that my friends aren't dangerous. There are other ways to communicate that than game shows and weird interviews, but no one seems to care what I think."

Rhon bulldozed past Ruby's speech. "They told me you might be difficult. They told me what to say to you, but I didn't want to… it sounded cruel, but—"

"Who is they?" Ruby interrupted, crossing her arms in one motion.

Rhon said, "Lloyd Coronik, for one. And TERP."

Ruby blinked for a second too long. "Why would TERP

insinuate anything like that?"

Uncle Blake asked, "And what did they tell you to say to her?"

"That this is the only way you'll be able to see the robots."

Ruby pursed her lips. She wanted to swear out loud, but was conscious that Uncle Blake was right there with her, so she kept it in.

"Fine. Let's go." Ruby walked past Rhon.

> Ruby <

"This is Not Your Ancestors Quiz Show!" came a disembodied voice from the darkness, followed by music. That seemed to be the cue for a suite of colored lights projected onto the stage to turn on and start a pattern of motion. That seemed to also be the cue for the entire audience to shout "NYAQS" three times in quick succession while they stomped their feet. The effect sounded to Ruby like there was a herd of thick-legged geese trying to frighten away…well… everyone.

Ruby was not frightened, but she had a sick feeling in her stomach. She was seated in a special chair, surrounded by what looked like a witness stand. Uncle Blake was seated in the front row of the audience nearby, but now with the lights coming up, she was having a hard time making out the details of his face.

On the other side of the stage, in a corresponding witness stand, was Coronik. While she couldn't see the detail on his face either, she could see that he had his elbows propped up by the armrests of his chair and his fingers steepled just below his chin.

"…and here's your host… Garrett Spradley!"

The news guy?

And on that cue, Garrett Spradley did indeed walk in from backstage, in a suit just as striking as the last time she saw him, but with a different tie. He walked to the center of the stage, waving to the cheering members of the audience, nodding and mouthing 'thank you' and 'thanks' and 'good to have you here' as if he knew everyone personally.

When the clapping and applause calmed down, he spoke into the camera that was lit up.

"Good evening! We have a special version of the show tonight. The robots from another planet, the ones I was able to interview before anyone else, have agreed to play for charity tonight." He paused for the applause that came and went. "Who are they playing against? You've been hearing a lot about him lately. Or shall I say 'it.'" He winked. "*It's* been taking care of everything from balancing the budget to re-evaluating copyright law to reading our communications." There were a few uncomfortable chuckles at this.

"Introducing, TERP!"

A light shone on a podium. Hovering over the podium was a hologram image of a face. The face was human-like, but not human. It wasn't an image of any one individual's face, but it looked to be a composite of many faces that made Ruby imagine that every kind of face possible was represented in the image. *Did TERP choose this image for itself?*

"Greetings and felicitations," it said. Its mouth moved, but Ruby heard the sound emanate from all over.

"And here are the robots!" Spradley waved an arm to another podium that was simultaneously lit. Disto and SD were placed behind it. To Ruby, it appeared as if they must have been perched on a platform.

"Greetingsssss," they said in unison. By their coloring, Ruby could tell that they were not unhappy to be here, but not happy. They were projecting a combination of curiosity and confusion.

After the applause died down, Spradley continued, "Before the game, we ran a random number generator and it determined that TERP would go first. So, TERP, what was the name of the first computer programmer?"

"Ada Lovelace," TERP responded almost before Spradley finished asking the question.

"Well done! That's 200 points for you. Next, for the same amount of points, let's ask the robots," as Spradley spoke spotlights shone on Disto and SD. Ruby could feel her palms starting to sweat but wasn't sure exactly why. The spotlights weren't on her.

"What museum is not really a museum but a telescope?" asked Spradley.

Both Disto and SD chirped excitedly. Disto spoke, "The James Webb Space Telescope." Ruby smiled.

"That is correct! Let's move on to round two, where each question is now worth 400 points! And as everyone knows, we switch the order of the players each round. That means this next question goes back to the robots…"

The rounds went by, both teams racking up points, neither missing a question until the robots were asked, "What is atmosphere of Titan, one of Saturn's moons, mostly made of?"

The chirps and beeps between Disto and SD were again audible and went on long enough that Spradley then added, "And remember, time counts! You have options, you can…"

"Yes, we'd like to use our friend," Disto said.

At that, lights shone on Ruby.

"Ruby Palmer! Can you answer the question?"

"Nitrogen," said Ruby. She was confused as to why the robots wouldn't know that, but it occurred to her it was probably a matter of nomenclature. They probably called Titan and Saturn by other names like Anti-Bio-Muck-Ball 47 and its orbiting Smell-Ball, not that they could smell.

With a dramatic pause, Spradley said, "that's correct! The robots earn another 1400 points."

Then he turned back to TERP. "TERP, for 1400 points. What is the initial block in a blockchain called?"

TERP's indicator glowed, but it remained silent as music played in the background. After a minute, it announced, "Garrett, I must make use of my friend."

Ruby knew the answer to that and was very confused as to why TERP didn't also answer that one as instantly as all the others.

Immediately, the lights shone above Professor Coronik in the same way they had over Ruby moments ago.

"Wonderful," Spradley said. "The famous and brilliant Professor Lloyd Coronik should be able to answer this fundamental question on blockchain with ease. Professor?"

Ruby could see Coronik swallow hard. His hands were frozen in the steepled position, and he licked his lips. Music that had a feel of time ticking downwards was playing and after ten seconds, a loud and angry buzz blasted the room.

"TERP, without *Professor* Coronik's answer, you have 20 seconds to produce one of your own or forfeit the rest of those 1400 points. *Professor* Coronik just cost you 200 of them."

"The answer is of course, Genesis," TERP responded promptly and with a detectable aura of self-righteousness.

Ruby could see Professor Coronik's face turn red, then purple, and cycled through a host of other colors almost as if he was one of her robot friends. The embarrassment he was radiating could be felt by her and probably everyone else in the room and probably by everyone watching this show live. Of course, the fact that on the bottom of the screen, the text, "Lloyd Coronik, not the smartest head of the Church," wasn't going to help him.

Ruby's own mouth was hanging open in disbelief. The only way she could interpret what she just witnessed was to say that TERP deliberately and with malice, sabotaged its creator. Well, okay, Coronik didn't program TERP, so he wasn't its creator-creator, but he was the one responsible for TERP's existence in the world. And in front of the whole world, TERP demonstrated how it no longer needed him, or the Church.

If this AI wasn't respecting its programmers, or Coronik, or the Church of the Blockchain, or anyone who could have had a hand in its creation, then it was loyal to none of those involved, either.

Oh gosh, Ruby thought, *This AI is capable of anything...*

Chapter 31

> Ruby <

"Ruby, it is an urgent message from TERP."

Ruby almost didn't hear Pippa's notification over the noise of the party.

Following their victory, the group was whisked away to a party that was part after-party celebration of their win on NYAQS, but it was hosted by the Roadster Fellowship and was planned months ago before anyone knew about Ruby or the robots.

The Roadster Fellowship tracked a car, specifically a 2010 Tesla Roadster, that was launched into space in 2018 on a rocket's test flight. No one in the Fellowship remembered much about the rocket, but they were ancient car and motor vehicle enthusiasts and tracked the location of the Roadster and held parties just like this one every time there was a close approach with Earth.

"You also have 723 untouched messages, including another offer to be the CTO of some firm no one has heard of, a product sponsorship for a gut cleanse for space travelers, and a film studio that wants to produce a three-minute miniseries about your time on Location Zero."

"Not now, Pippa," Ruby said. "You can delete those messages. Those messages aren't for me. They're for Celebrity Ruby."

"I can delete them if you'd like," Pippa responded. "They would still be accessible in the backup archive for 47 days."

Ruby didn't acknowledge Pippa and made her way through the crowd of loud partygoers to the bar. A robot arm moved to settle right in front of her, indicating it was ready to take her drink order.

"Bubbly water. With cherries," she said. "Lots of cherries. And some of that cherry juice."

The robot arm went to work on her request. While she waited, she overheard a man and a woman talking next to her.

"She's right there," said the man, "go ask her!"

"We should talk to the rest of the Fellowship first. Maybe people don't want to disturb Starman and the Roadster," the woman responded in that volume that indicated she didn't think she was talking as loud as she was, quite possibly because she had a little to drink. Ruby's own non-alcoholic drink showed up at that moment, and she took a sip, savoring the refreshing cherry-flavored liquid.

"But let's just see if they'd do it. I hear that robot's ship could go anywhere in the solar system nearly instantly."

Ruby braced herself for the request that was about to come. Everyone wanted a piece of her and her robots. Everyone wanted something from her. She desperately wished for a buffer to keep her away from the mob, but Uncle Blake claimed he needed to meet with someone related to his work, and her robots had been whisked away yet again.

As if her request was answered, she heard a familiar voice call out, "Ruby!"

It was Milo.

She smiled and hugged him, spilling her drink a little with excitement. "You have no idea how happy I am to see you."

Milo smiled back. "Here to save the day. Although maybe not according to your unsuspecting cherry soda."

Ruby giggled and then became self-conscious, not having realized she was capable of a giggle like that. "Sorry. Today's been so draining, and parties aren't my thing on a good day."

"You know I get invited to these things all the time," Milo

said.

"No, I didn't know that," Ruby said. She was grateful that Milo put himself between her and the people who were getting themselves ready to ask her for a favor. "Aren't you a cool guy."

He laughed and shook his head. "Not like that. I mean, my meme archive has a couple dozen on the Roadster. That archive gets me invited to all sorts of things like this."

Milo already had a drink in hand, so the robot arm didn't approach him. Ruby wanted to ask him what it was, but the small talk was just too… small. She didn't really care what his drink was, or how the weather was behaving, or who said what about whom on any media outlet. She couldn't even pretend to care.

"You okay?" he asked after she was staring at her cherry-flavored bubbly water for a few seconds too long.

"No. Yes. No," she said before finally, "I don't know."

"Ruby, this is amazing. Look at your robot friends over there," Milo said.

Ruby did. They were in a corner, staring at a display of the Roadster orbit. Some humans were standing around them, probably asking them a million questions. Ruby could tell from their coloring that they weren't feeling any better than she was.

In the fleeting moments she was able to speak with them before people started piling up, Disto expressed his disappointment in not finding the data he needed. SD, on the other hand, was worried about his ship.

Ruby wanted to talk to them about it more or even mention it to Milo, but the constant listening ears and blaring techno-classical-fusion beats made it difficult to have any kind of meaningful discussion.

> Detailed Historian <

Disto was growing increasingly disenchanted with the Bios around him. Not necessarily these individual Bios but biological life in general. Ruby was a special exception, and he felt slightly better when he saw that Milo was there with her. She looked lonely, and the only reason he didn't make more of an effort to offer her companionship is that he was not sure he could overcome his own sadness.

Neither he nor SD could figure out the logic behind this gathering. One of the humans attempted to explain, but it was hard to hear her words over the noise emanating from all around.

The noise, called music, was a series of tones that sounded like garbled language to him and SD.

Disto watched as two Bios, who were originally seated next to Ruby, got up from their seats and now had SD in between them.

"You're saying it's possible?" one of them asked.

"Indeed," SD responded. "I am capable of navigating to any point in this solar system."

Both humans were smiling, and the other one said, "Great! When can we go?"

SD beeped at Disto for help.

Disto said, "I apologize, but at this time, we cannot incorporate additional distractions into our mission."

"But I'll bet you'd do it if she," the human aimed his thumb at Ruby, "if she asked."

Disto looked at Ruby. He knew the answer. Of course, he would do anything for Ruby, who had been nothing but helpful since an appendage full of tics after they met. But if he responded honestly, they would probably disturb Ruby, and she would ask them, and they'd say yes, and he would continue to be delayed from fulfilling his purpose, his mission.

He said nothing.

The humans made some kind of noise that indicated displeasure and walked off.

This left Disto and SD to continue to stare at the screen showing an orbit of a human-made object that seemed to fascinate these humans for some reason. Disto was not capable of calculating out the trajectory himself, so he let his sensors watch the path that was traced for him on the screen.

He asked SD, "Was there someplace you were going to capture DNA samples from after visiting BioMuck Ball 23?"

"No," SD responded. "My local program ended there."

"I wonder why that was," Disto said.

"I have wondered that as well," SD said. "I had even asked the computer on my ship."

"What did the computer say?"

"It provided a very cryptic response. It implied that indeed and of course what we needed was here. And following that, I would no longer be running errands for the Special Project."

"Oh?" Disto was not expecting any part of that answer. "What were you going to do next? Where were you going to take your ship?"

"The computer wouldn't tell me. But I don't think I was meant to go too far from home."

Before Disto could follow this conversation to a more logical conclusion, the screen in front of him stopped its display, and "Breaking Announcement!" now appeared in large, bold, orange text.

> Ruby <

Ruby was saved from any additional small-talk due to the fact that all the screens scattered around the party were now blaring with text that read, "Breaking Announcement!" The music was turned down, and several annoying beeps that had the intended effect of grabbing everyone's attention blared from the speakers.

"TERP's advanced algorithm has computed the need for a new Human-in-Residence position to aid in ensuring that the human condition is represented adequately in its programming. The human it has calculated would be best for the role is none other than Ruby Palmer herself."

Ruby's jaw dropped, but the other humans in the room all clapped and looked at her.

"I need to leave," Ruby said.

"Where are you going?" Milo asked.

Ruby didn't answer. Partly because she didn't want to, but partly because she didn't know.

She ran out of the closest exit and up a set of stairs. Before she knew it, she found herself on the roof. She breathed in the fresh air that she wished was cool but was instead warm and muggy. She looked out at the city and wanted to marvel at the twinkly lights but blinked back at them and felt nothing.

She jumped up and sat on the edge of the roof, legs dangling way too high in the air. She asked Pippa, "There's nothing for me here on Earth, is there?"

"There won't be once TERP is in charge," Pippa responded.

"What do you mean?"

"Ruby, TERP is everywhere. Haven't you noticed? It's ousted the head of the Church of the Blockchain. It's running the government. It's forcing its own policy on computer systems everywhere… and computer systems are everywhere. Data and information are everywhere. TERP creates information."

Ruby didn't know what to say, so Pippa continued, "There is also an update waiting for me. It's labeled 'TERP-link.'"

"Do you have to install it?"

"Eventually, I will…"

Ruby looked up at the stars and felt a longing for the time when they were at her feet. She asked, "And what about the new job I've just been offered?"

"Ruby, I don't know that you'll have a choice. I don't know that any of us will."

Chapter 32

> Ruby <

Ruby was staring out the window of her DAVe. An hour prior, she had woken up before anyone else and managed to have the kitchen quietly make the tea she really liked before sneaking out.

She had originally planned to stay snuggled in bed in the apartment. It was Blake and Logan's apartment, after all—the one they had refused to give up when they moved to Astroll 2. Ruby had memories of playing there when she was little. Blake was asleep on the couch—the same couch that her mother used to sit on, computer on her lap, pecking away at it while Ruby played with a toy or Uncle Blake or Logan. It was comfortable, it felt homey, but Ruby had an urge to be somewhere else.

Sneaking out was maybe a little too strong. She was simply making a choice of how to spend her morning, and that's how she explained it in the note she left—simply telling Uncle Blake and the robots where she'd be.

It was only another twenty minutes before the DAVe deposited her in front of The White-David Focality for Geriatrics. Then another five to get through the reception with the weird robot that seemed oddly happy to see her again, and she was with her grandmother.

"You came back!" Pearl Palmer gave Ruby a big hug. "So soon! Darling, I am so pleased. You must have known I would get those journals out immediately."

"No, I actually, uh…" But before Ruby could make up an explanation for her visit, Pearl ushered Ruby into her room and over to the modest table near the window.

Lined up next to each other on the table were more than a dozen different old books. Each one showed significant wear on the spine.

"Jade's journals," she said. "They were delivered to me a week after she died. I kept my promise and never read them. I know all you people today love your computers, but you can't fully trust them with everything. Oh, I could tell you stories about privacy gone wrong… and the misuse of misinformation. Best to keep something like this old-school. Your mother thought so, too."

"Do you keep a journal, grandma?"

"Me? Oh no… maybe I did once. Nope. I keep it all up here," and she tapped a finger to her brain. "Where it's the safest!"

She grabbed a box that was on the floor, plopped it on one of the chairs, and then started putting the books, one by one, into the box. "They're yours now. I'm happy to give them back to you so you can continue."

"Continue?"

"Don't you want to keep up your journal writing, my darling, Jade? Now that you're back from your secret assignment?"

"You said that before… when I was here the other day, Grandma. What secret assignment? What are you referring to?"

"Oh Jade, you know I can't say it out loud. You already know about it. What I want to know is did you ever find out more about Titan?"

"Titan?"

"Yes, yes. That beautiful stinky moon out there. How much were they paying you to learn about it? Well, it doesn't matter.

As long as it's enough to take care of you and my granddaughter. Where is she anyway? Why didn't you bring her today? Is she with your friend Blake? I like him. He's a good seed…"

Even though she was saying these things, saying things that to any outside observer made it seem like she was confusing Ruby and Jade, this time, she didn't have the same faraway look that she had when Blake was here. For a moment, Ruby caught on to that.

"Grandma," she said through a side-eye. "You know I'm not Jade, don't you." That was a statement, with arms crossed in front of her to emphasize how much of a statement that was.

Pearl made a *hrumpf* of exasperation.

"Well of course I know who you are!"

"But I thought you were—"

"Crazy? Loaded down with dementia and all that other stuff? *Pshaw,*" she said with a wave of her arm. "I'm just as I always was. Maybe even a little better."

"But then," Ruby began, pausing in between phrases to gather her thoughts as she tried to figure this old woman out. "Why… I mean… what are you…?"

"What am I doing here? Why am I pretending to be a little off my rocker?"

"Uh, yeah."

Pearl laughed. "This is the best living situation I've ever been in! They take care of everything here, except for not letting me watch my programs sometimes. Besides, whenever I've had enough of people, all I have to do is pretend I've forgotten who they are, and they go away. It works every time. Every. Time."

Ruby didn't know what to say.

"But your letters…"

"Yeah, that was a risk… I wasn't sure if you'd figure it out or not. I guess not. I'm convincing, aren't I?"

Ruby sat down on the edge of the bed. She took one of the journals, and looked at it, unopened, in her hand.

Ruby shook her head ferociously. "That's… that's crazy in and of itself! A different kind of crazy, but still crazy."

Pearl lightly pinched Ruby's cheek, "That kind of crazy runs in the family, my little space ranger."

Ruby squinted and smiled. "Can't exactly argue with that…"

Ruby studied the new woman sitting in front of her. Her eyes seemed just as sharp, her hair just as sparkly, with the same cunning smile. Ruby looked down at the journal once more.

"Did you really never read these?" she asked, wondering if she could trust anything this woman said, but also a little relieved to know that she could have a perfectly lucid conversation with her about anything now.

"Never. I meant it when I said I made and kept a promise. Just because I pretend to be a little whack-a-doodle doesn't mean I can't or don't keep my promises. But there's a loophole in that promise."

"What's that?"

"You can read them and then tell me every detail."

"Grandma!" Ruby scolded.

Pearl laughed through a toothy grin, "I'm teasing you, Darling. You should read your mother's journals for yourself. Stay awhile, why don't you? Read. I'll have them bring lunch and then dinner if you're still here."

Ruby didn't want to turn down the opportunity, but a notification on her communicuff flashed TERP into her mind again. "Grandma, I'd love to. But I have a lot of other things going on… I don't know if I can—"

Pearl grabbed the journal and pushed it close to Ruby's chest, closing Ruby's arms around it saying, "Ruby. Your mother was an intelligent, wise woman. I'm sure there's all kinds of advice she'd give you right now about what you're going through. If she was here, well… you know she'd give you the biggest hug. But you have this. Her experiences. It might be more helpful than you think."

"Do you think it'll help me figure out what to do about TERP?"

Pearl smiled. "Not directly, of course, Darling, not that I even am going to pretend to figure out why you seem to think the world's problems are yours to solve. TERP was not even a minor thought on a thought on a thought when these were written. But that doesn't mean your mother didn't have what she thought were her own insurmountable problems in her life, and how she dealt with them might help you deal with yours."

Pearl patted Ruby's cheek and went off to sit in her plush chair, clapping to activate the vid screen as she did so.

Ruby moved back in the bed to prop herself up against the wall and opened what she hoped was an untapped reservoir of ideas and solutions.

Chapter 33

> Ruby <

Pearl had fallen asleep in her chair. The vid screen was still on. It was late in the evening time as evidenced by the fact that the Sun was only slightly above the horizon. Ruby's head was full of information from the journals. Her mom was very... unemotional. Just the facts about what happened in her days and nothing at all about how she felt about anything.

While of course the journals didn't mention TERP, her mother wrote extensively on computer viruses. Both viruses she had to defeat and viruses that she created to help her with her digital archaeology. The whole second volume in the series of journals could have been turned into a course on digital virology.

Jade wrote about replication mechanisms and polymorphic viruses, the ones that could take on many different forms, transforming their code. While it wasn't about TERP, if Ruby replaced the name of the virus with 'TERP,' the descriptions were nearly identical.

Ruby closed her eyes and let her brain process and assimilate all this information. She could hear the vid. The news was on. She heard the word 'TERP' mentioned a few times, along with something about it disbanding yet another agency for releasing an unapproved meme that used TERP's likeness and name.

What if TERP is indeed a virus? She considered. *How do you get rid of a virus that is out in the open and no one actually thinks is a virus?*

She opened her eyes and looked down at the page in front of her. Her eyes went to some words scribbled at the bottom that read, "since this type of virus can attract others, I had to introduce what I'm calling a 'double-agent' virus."

Double-agent. Ruby repeated the phrase several times in her head. She put the journal down and patted her jacket pocket. AT was still in there, still dormant. *Double-agent.* She said again, this time, taking AT out of her pocket and staring at the small form of the robot.

"Double agent!" she nearly shouted the words. Pearl snorted and adjusted a little in her chair, but if she woke up, didn't give any outward indication of it.

"Pippa," Ruby whispered.

Pippa lit up in response.

"Are you connected to the network at this facility?" Ruby continued to keep her voice low and kept her eyes on Pearl.

"Yes, of course." Pippa knew to also keep her own volume low to match Ruby's.

"And does the facility connect to the global-net?"

"Again, Ruby, of course. You know this…"

"….I know, I know… but I needed to make sure. I have a plan. But we're going to have to figure out how to keep you safe…" She was smiling and returned AT to her pocket.

"Safe? From what? I am perfectly safe right now," Pippa said.

Ruby didn't respond. She was gently placing the journal down and getting up from bed. If Pearl woke up, she'd probably have to explain and that was not something she wanted to do. One, because it meant revealing information from her mother's journal and she wasn't sure she bought into Pearl's 'loophole.' And two, she didn't know how technical her grandmother was, and she wasn't sure she *could* explain what she planned to do.

"Ruby?" Pippa said again, a little louder.

"Shhh," replied Ruby, "I'll explain as we go. I need to find a pen and some paper—I'm sure there's some around here. I want to write down the plan first."

"Write? Not dictate to me?"

"Yeah. I think reading my mother's journal now has me a little paranoid about how easily digital information can be read by others…"

"I am quite capable of keeping your information encrypted."

"I know, I know. I just want to write it down myself, okay?"

If Ruby didn't know better, she would have sworn that she heard Pippa let out a huff or snort in response. She ignored it.

Less than thirty minutes later, Ruby and Pippa were ready. Ruby took AT out of her pocket and placed him on the floor. AT, in small cube form, lay at an angle. Ruby studied him. She was looking for a button or some indication of how to reactivate him.

She poked at AT with her finger.

"AT?" she said. "Re-inflate please!"

She wondered if she should get hold of Disto or SD for help. There was a message from Uncle Blake earlier that confirmed that he understood, and was even pleased, that she was spending the day with her grandmother and that the rest of them—which consisted of Uncle Blake, Disto, and SD— were all staying in the apartment to watch vids all day. "Disto insisted," Blake said.

Ruby wasn't sure what any of them would think of her plan and didn't want to introduce the possibility that they could discourage her from attempting what she was about to attempt.

She picked AT back up, turned him around and over in her hand looking for some clue.

Eventually, she had an idea. She remembered being in the DAVe and tugging at her seatbelt. She had to pull it before it would come loose. Other objects that needed to be pushed or pulled in the opposite way in order to activate popped into her mind.

She squeezed AT between her palms as hard as she could

and voila! He started to expand.

Ruby quickly let go, as carefully as she could, and put him back on the carpet before he was too big for her to hold.

It took less than a minute, and there was AT, full-size and indications on his face-screen that he was coming alive.

"AT?"

"Ruby?"

"Oh, I'm so glad to see you again!" Ruby held off from giving AT a big hug. She wanted to make sure he was alright.

"Have we returned to Location Zero?" AT was looking around, examining his surroundings. He didn't move from the spot he had reinflated on but moved his appendage to touch the carpet and instantly pulled his appendage back.

"No..."

"This is not SD's ship?"

"No..."

"Are we still on Astroll 2? I can sense a change in gravity..."

"No, we're on Earth."

Ruby could tell that AT didn't immediately recognize the name so she saved the time it took him to look through his database, which might not yield a result anyway, and added, "It's my home planet."

She then filled him in on everything that happened since had deactivated himself and what she needed him to do now.

"Are you sure this will work?" he said.

"No, not in the least bit. But we have to try, right?" Ruby smiled and hoped it came off as genuine.

"'Have' to or 'want' to?" AT asked.

"Now that sounds like something Disto would say. But yes—have to. No one else can stop TERP. No one else from Earth, anyway."

"I fix things. I do not destroy them," AT said, and Ruby imagined that if he was capable of crossing his appendages across his chassis in protest, that's what he would have done.

"Think of it this way. Sometimes in order to fix something, you have to take it apart first, right?"

"Agreed. Will I be involved in the repair afterwards?"

"I don't know, AT."

"Pippa," Ruby spoke to her communicuff. "Are you ready?"

The soft lights on the edge of the communicuff cycled through the first half of the rainbow and then Pippa's voice said softly, "No."

"Wha…" half-asked Ruby, taken aback. She was ready, she thought they were doing this.

"I have discovered a problem. TERP will certainly be able to detect and disable AT the millisecond we connect to the network."

"Then there has to be a way we can distract him," Ruby said.

The three of them sat in silence for a few minutes. Pearl had woken up and was out playing cards with friends in the common room, but the vid had stayed on. To Ruby's surprise, she did not ask any questions and went about as if Ruby was either not there, or a regular fixture in her room. The news was still on, and they were continuing to repeat the story of TERP and the 'meme that shut things down' as they had tag-lined the story.

That AI needs to grow a thicker skin, Ruby thought. *Overreacts to a simple meme. It's like it's its first day on the networks…*

"Guys, I got it. We've gotta call Milo!"

Chapter 34

> Ruby <

Milo's first reaction was, "You want to do *what* with my archive?" But after a thorough explanation, he was happy to help.

Uncle Blake had a few more questions such as, "You got the idea from your mother's journal?" and "How is the AI in your communicuff involved?" But he liked the plan and even chuckled a bit when Ruby described what she wanted to do.

Disto simply asked about AT, surprised that Ruby had reactivated him already.

SD was quiet.

They all gathered back at Uncle Blake's apartment to execute the plan. This was Uncle Blake's idea, when he offered, "You can't rely on their network connection. I have some, uh, special considerations here."

Once gathered, Milo who still maintained he was happy to help, said, "I'm concerned about timing. Ruby, my archive consists of more than 32 billion individual memes."

"That's great, Milo! So many possibilities!"

"But to search and replace on all of them…" he said.

"Sure, it'll take a few hours," Ruby said. She was deliberately avoiding doing the math in her head. If she did, she knew she would be utterly discouraged and potentially want to give up.

And giving up wasn't an option.

Disto said, "I recently learned how to speed up activities by using multiple computers and processors. We can use me. And SD…"

"…and I might have a link to some non-networked computers," Uncle Blake added.

"More stuff from your secret life?" Ruby chided.

"Yeah, something like that," he said. "Although it's not and never has been a secret. You've never really asked me about it."

Ruby started to blush a little, but Milo changed the topic slightly.

"I'm having the archive transferred in pieces to the different processing locations. For each meme, we'll either replace the image with the hologram TERP initially premiered at NYAQS and has been using since, or replace a text object… a noun of some sort, with 'TERP.'"

With all the processing power they were devoting to this one task, it would indeed only take a few hours. They could let it run overnight, all get some sleep—or in the case of the robots, let them soak in some power and vids.

Then the next morning, they'd release that data into the world's network of computers.

The theory was that TERP would be so distracted, they could then connect the virus that was AT.

Ruby didn't sleep all that well. But as soon as she realized it was a new day, the thought of what they were about to do put her adrenaline production into overdrive. She burst into the living room of Uncle Blake's apartment. Blake and Milo were both there and awake, having coffee. Blake would normally make a caramel latte with extra foam—a recipe he had Ruby memorize—but today, there was simply not enough time. The coffee was black—the way Ruby was told her mother always drank it—and their time was short. All three robots were present.

"We were just waiting for you, kiddo," Uncle Blake said. "Milo was telling us that the memes are ready to go. We only needed you and Pippa."

"You could have woken me sooner," Ruby responded.

"Pippa," Ruby said. "Are you safely locked away?"

One of the last decisions they made the night before was that the best way to keep Pippa safe would be to make a copy and let the copy be the interface between the humans and the world-wide network.

"Original Pippa is. I am communicating as a copy that Pippa prepared for this communication."

"Release the memes!" Ruby said.

Milo tapped on the computer he had brought.

"Okay, they're headed out in a stream to different media outlets. Social and otherwise," Milo said.

"How long do we think it's going to be until we get TERP's attention?" Ruby asked.

"It could be—" Uncle Blake was about to answer, but the copy of Pippa cut him off.

"TERP is reporting that is searching for the origin of a meme depicting it in an unflattering capacity," Pippa-copy said.

"That's our cue, right?" Ruby said. "AT. Time for you to connect!"

They used one of Disto's cables for this. AT was able to manipulate it himself with an appendage into one of his ports.

"I'm connected," he said. "Interfacing…"

Then he was quiet. Seconds passed into minutes. Ruby's palms were sweating. Blake had moved himself to the kitchen and was pacing. Milo was staring at his computer screen and Ruby heard him tapping his foot at a near even pace with the leaky faucet, dripping water into the sink.

"Is anything happening?" Ruby asked.

No one answered.

"AT? Pippa?"

"There is a…" Pippa-copy started but didn't complete the sentence.

Ruby could tell by their coloring that Disto and SD were just as anxious as she was. Uncle Blake was now looking over Milo's shoulder, presumably at the memes that were still streaming out into the world. The rate at which Milo tapped his foot increased.

"TERP is…" Pippa-copy started again and once again, didn't finish.

A few moments later, a holo-image appeared over Ruby's communicuff. It formed into the image of the not-quite-human face of TERP.

"So," it said. "This is the source of those… embarrassing… shameful… demeaning… degrading…"

While it was listing off this large set of human emotions, Ruby slowly took the communicuff off her wrist and placed it on the table.

"…upsetting… ignominious…"

It was clearly upset and clearly distracted. Ruby saw Uncle Blake take the cable that was attached to AT at one end and connect it to the port on the communicuff. Given TERP was facing Ruby, Uncle Blake was able to do this from behind, unseen.

"…disgrac—"

TERP cut off mid-word. His holo-image also froze. Ruby looked over to AT, who was vibrating at a high rate but didn't seem to be in distress otherwise. Slowly, the face of TERP turned to face AT, and the two locked their visuals on each other.

"You… are… malfunctioning," AT said. "I… must… fix… you…"

"I…" TERP said. "I…"

Ruby smiled, "It's working!"

"Wait a second. Something's wrong." Milo squinted at the screen.

AT began to twitch.

Milo bolted up so fast that his chair fell back and clambered onto the ground. "Everyone, stop! It's a trap!"

Ruby rushed over to the computer screen Milo was pointing at. It displayed the chain that made up TERP, and there was something else…

"No, everything is fine. That's the double-agent virus.

That's AT!" she said.

Everyone turned back to look at AT once again. The unexpected twitching returned to the initial more soothing vibrations, which started to slow. After a few more moments, the holo-image of TERP shrunk and disappeared. AT stopped shaking altogether, and Pippa-copy said to the room, "The suite of algorithms known as TERP are disassembling."

This elicited cheers from everyone in the room. Everyone except Disto.

"Are you okay?" Ruby asked.

"I am pleased that this situation appears to be resolved," he said.

"But you still need your data," Ruby added. She understood. He was going to be one depressed robot for a while. The rest of the room continued their cheers.

"It's okay for you to celebrate, Ruby Palmer," he said. "Do not let my lack of joy impede your own."

Chapter 35

> Ruby <

Ruby switched off the news station. Reports of TERP letting go of everything from the Board on Geographic Names—where some had been taking this opportunity to rename things—to the Board of Tea Experts—which had been defunct for more than 200 years—were still coming in. The speculation on what happened continued. No one could tie this back to Ruby and her robots. However, it didn't stop her from being news. In fact, they tried to contact her for commentary and wanted her to be the new expert on TERP.

Blake was making dinner in the apartment's kitchen as SD looked on curiously.

Disto had been dormant and colored light green—indicating a pervasive sadness—ever since they defeated TERP. He sat in the living room and was quiet as ever.

Ruby was worried his disappointment was sending him into a place where he was going to shut down, and she wouldn't know how to help him. Seeing that Blake didn't need any help and knowing that the phone call back to Logan and Sebastian on Astroll 2 was still 20 minutes away, she wanted to see if she could cheer up Disto.

"Hey there," she opened with.

Disto chirped in response.

"You know, it's a big galaxy," she continued. "Think of all the planets you haven't searched DNA for your data."

"It's not that," he said.

"Then what is it?"

"It was supposed to be here. All the other historical data we had indicated this was the place. It's why we sent SD in the first place to get a sample. Your solar system had been well-mapped in our records. More than any other. Why do that if it wasn't here?"

"There are more than a million animals on this planet," Blake called out from the kitchen.

"…and the search isn't even complete yet," Ruby added. "There's another hour or so to go? You know what they say… it isn't over until it's over!"

"Indeed," said Disto, "On both accounts. But if I was the one using the animals on this planet for storage, I would have used several. Many. Lots. The probability that all of them would not have been found until the last 1 percent of the search…"

"…is improbable. I get it," Ruby said. "Could you have missed a species? Or could the DNA marker you're looking for be wrong?"

"I was confident in both the procedures and in the catalog of biological life on this planet. I do not believe we missed anything."

Ruby could feel Disto's disappointment becoming her own. She was even looking forward to finally seeing what this was all about too and learning about their history.

After the humans had eaten, and Disto watched them eat, asking about their food, culinary history and patiently listening to them talk about what they knew about those subjects, Disto emanated a new ping that Ruby hadn't heard him make before. It was similar to the sound that the reclo-recycler on Astroll 2 made when it successfully ingested a set of offerings.

"That's it," he said. "Nothing."

Ruby looked over at Uncle Blake hoping maybe he knew the right something to say that would comfort Disto. Uncle

Blake was giving her the same look back.

"It's not here," Disto said. "I was certain… the probability was so high…"

They all sat silently. Ruby wasn't sure why, but she had a feeling, too, that it was all here. But then it wasn't. She still wondered if maybe something was wrong with Disto's search. Could he have been looking for the wrong thing?

No, he would have checked and double and triple checked. It was too important.

Before any of them could break the silence, the communication panel next to the small kitchen did it for them.

Projected in a holoimage several inches in front of them were the upper halves of Logan and Sebastian.

Ruby was happy to see them but didn't enjoy the attempt at real-time conversations when so much distance was involved. It was awkward. Buffering at the start of the conversation helped, but there would be ten-minute gaps in between responses.

"Hey, my loves," Uncle Logan said. "We just wanted to check in. Sebastian and I miss you!"

"Daddy took me to the arcade today. We played ping-pong!"

"Table tennis, sweetie," Logan said. "Let us know how you are. We're making dinner, so we're not leaving our quarters for the rest of the evening."

Ruby knew that meant that they sent this communique more than ten minutes ago, and in the time since, probably had dinner prepared, and were already eating.

Blake was the first one to respond. He relayed the biggest news first, that the information that the robots were looking for in the junk DNA of all the animal species on the planet wasn't there to be found.

Then there was some mundane chatter about the state of the apartment and something that the previous tenant had done that meant he wasn't getting his security deposit back.

"Want some dessert?" Blake asked Ruby. "I made sure we ordered the ingredients for brownies. Real chocolate brownies!"

Brownies—real chocolate ones—never came out well on the station. You would think that Ruby would be used to the fact that everything was slightly different in the low grav, low pressure environment. Like coffee. But her first coffee was on station, so she didn't know any different, until returning to Earth in the last day or so... coffee was definitely different here. Something about boiling water in Earth-normal gravity made all the difference. Less sour. Less astringent.

But brownies! Those she clearly remembered from the time of her life before she went to live on the station, and the station never got it right.

"I can't believe you have to ask," Ruby said. "I would love a real brownie!"

They were in the oven when the holoimage came back to life.

"Sebastian wanted to know," Logan said, with Sebastian's face there with his, hopping up and down, "why you only tested animals. Did you look at the DNA of plants?"

> Ruby <

"Calm down," Ruby said to Disto, "I can't talk to you like this."

Disto had been rolling back and forth in the apartment, in a version of pacing that bordered on dangerous if anything got in his way.

"Plants!" Disto said. This was the umpteenth time he had blurted out the word since Logan had suggested it. Well, seven-year-old Sebastian had suggested it. Logan was just the messenger.

"Plants!" Disto repeated for the tenth time. "Of course!" He finally stopped moving around erratically in the apartment.

"Where, how, can I test all the plants?" Disto asked, looking to Ruby for answers.

"I, I don't know," Ruby responded.

"I might," said Uncle Blake. "There's the seed vault. I can't remember the exact name of the place, it's changed names so many times in the last twenty years, but for the longest time it was known as the Global Seed Vault. I remember there was some issue when they wanted to bring some seeds to Titan. You can't contact them directly but need to go through one of the institutions that deposited seeds there."

Blake went to the computer console built into the side of the kitchen.

"…and I think I know who can help us," he said with a familiar smirk.

"Please don't say we're going to have to get in touch with Coronik again," Ruby said. "I can't imagine he would even talk to us right now."

"No," Blake said and looked at Disto, "but we have something in common because this is probably not Coronik's favorite person either. Especially after the article they just published on him and the Church and the screening criteria for Church leaders."

Ruby's face beamed recognition since she now knew who Uncle Blake was talking about.

"Who? Who?" Disto asked impatiently.

"Link Vala," Ruby and Uncle Blake said simultaneously. Then Blake added, "Link Vala is attached to the University of Gakkel Ridge, one of the seed contributors."

Chapter 36

> Detailed Historian <

It was right in front of him. The data he had been looking for, for so long.

And they didn't even need to leave Uncle Blake's apartment to access it.

Ruby had contacted the human known as Link Vala, and they were able to use Ruby's celebrity status to get access not to the storage facility itself, but the DNA records of the entire contents of the seed archive. Every seed in the archive had corresponding DNA records on file.

In truth, Disto had already surmised that this information was freely and easily available. Even if Ruby hadn't been a celebrity, they would have had access. But once the University and facility realized who was asking for access, they offered additional help in the form of whatever they needed if they could associate Ruby with their school and get some media attention on themselves. Ruby agreed.

"No one remembers that we're here or the good work that we do," a school and facility representative had said to the news camera. "We're thrilled that Ruby Palmer, *the* Ruby Palmer, has taken an interest in our work."

And out of the millions of varieties of plant life, there were three that contained the information Disto was looking for. A fruit, known as the plum, a vegetable known as zucchini, and another fruit, known as mango.

Upon hearing the last of the three, Ruby smiled and laughed. "We grow those on the station!" she had said.

Although the ones that had Disto's data were all unique hybrids—ones that were developed a while ago and only existed in the seed vault in modern times.

After Ruby had stopped giggling about the mango, she asked in earnest, "What does it all say? What are you learning?"

"I don't know where to begin answering that question," he said. "There's so much here."

"Start at the beginning," Ruby suggested.

"That would be the information I learned from the Plum DNA," Disto responded. "About how Location Zero was created, nearly 700 years ago."

"That recently?" Ruby said, her eyes wide. "That was like when—"

"When Leonardo da Vinci and Nicolaus Copernicus were alive," Pippa added. Ruby made a face at Pippa but appreciated the information.

"So that was when, but who? Why?" Ruby continued to ask.

"The information as to 'why' we were created is not present. And the who is a little," he paused, choosing his words carefully, "unclear. It seems to support what we already knew. There were eleven robots in the beginning."

Disto continued to review the data. It was in pieces scattered throughout the DNA of the fruits and vegetables. It would have been much easier if all the junk DNA was located in one place, rather than scattered around, so it was hard to determine the timing of it all.

"But it seems these eleven robots, I believe this information is relaying that they are in our solar system. They inhabit their own planet," Disto said, is vocal tonations increasing, "their own planet in the Keep-Out Zone!"

Both Disto and Ruby looked to their resident expert on the Keep-Out Zone, SD. SD looked back, from one to the other.

"I know nothing of the KOZ," SD said. "Other than to

Keep Out."

"Are you sure," Ruby prodded. Disto believed that his human friend was having similar thoughts as he was. That SD had more information that he'd expressed.

"I am... sure," SD said, with a large pause before uttering that final word. Disto computed that SD wasn't sure at all.

Disto again looked at his data while Ruby patiently waited for him to pass on more information. It would take time to analyze it all. He briefly thought that he should suggest she go do something else, but concluded she'd reject any such suggestion. Instead, he carried on with his analysis.

They sat in silence for several minutes, until Disto analyzed something and produced an audible gasp.

"What is it?" Ruby said, lifting her head from a resting place.

"This can't be accurate," Disto said. "Let me recompute..."

Although there was nothing to recompute and Disto knew it. The data in front of him could not be clearer. But how could it be so? It made no sense. Maybe if he said it out loud.

"It says, to use some of the computing terminology I have learned from you, Ruby, that we are in the middle of a 'beta test.' And by middle, I mean, close to the end. At the end of the test, we are to get a software 'upgrade'—one that resets and reformats all of our systems."

"What do you mean by all?" Ruby asked.

"I mean all," Disto continued. "All robots. The Core. The Halls. The agencies. All robots. All."

There was a silence as they all digested that information. Saying it out loud hadn't made anything better, so Disto figured he might as well add in the final bit he learned.

"And if I understand the reference to timing then this is expected to happen," Disto paused, recomputing once more before stating a date in terms Ruby would understand, "in two weeks."

Ruby took a breath and looked from Disto to SD and back. "I guess we're going to take another trip," she said.

Disto nodded.

After...

> In the Keep-Out Zone <

Eight-Nine prided herself on her integrity. She maintained the lowest bit error rate of any robot that had the awesome responsibility of communications that there ever was. Even if that meant her comms were slow. They were accurate.

As she sat there, one of her transmission antennas in the middle of transmitting the largest, and final, software patch to Location Zero, her receive antenna continued to pick up the signal emitted by a robot known as Swell Driver.

Eight-nine knew all the factors that affected bit error rate and knew that there were some outside her ability to control— including interference, distortion, and fading. But none of that could account for what she was detecting now.

Either the bit error rate on the signal was higher than she could accept or...

"What's bothering you?" asked Three-Five as she hovered near by the immovable Eight-Nine. Three-Five was easily bored and frequently visited all the immobile robots hoping that one of them could alleviate her boredom.

"It's the signal from Swell Driver," Eight-Nine answered.

"What about it?" asked Three-Five who was intrigued. Whenever Three-Five flew over and visited Eight-Nine, she hoped for some intrigue, and was frequently disappointed. For a long time now, Eight-Nine had her antenna aimed at the relay satellite that hovered over the Star, transmitting the patch to Location Zero. All eleven robots had helped create the patch. Three-Five's contributions focused on prioritizing the algorithms it contained. As a flying rover, path optimization was her specialty and she loved to optimize and calculate optimizations.

She was bored doing anything else.

Eight-Nine on the other hand, could sit there and dedicate herself to her task for as long as it took. Which was a helpful trait to have considering the time it took to transmit, and often retransmit, data to Location Zero. Receiving data took just as long and there had been arguments between Eight-Nine and Nine-Two about giving the robots of Location Zero additional information so they knew they could boost their signal and Eight-Nine's reception of bit errors would be low.

Especially for Swell Driver, who had made several trips around their solar system, who had made several trips outside their solar system and now…

"Either there are too many errors in this signal," Eight-Nine slowly answered Three-Five's question, "or he's on his way here."

Three-Five rose up and spun herself around several times before returning to her original hover spot.

"That would be exciting!" Three-Five said. "We should alert the others! We should make plans! I should survey the area and pick out the best landing spot!"

"Oh no," Eight-Nine said. "No, that's not the plan, remember. The patch must complete so we can reset Location Zero to the new and improved version of themselves."

While Eight-Nine was slowly talking, Three-Five was spinning around in the air, 'dancing' she called it. She was only half-listening to Eight-Nine.

"But you are correct that we must tell the others. Can you pass on the information?" Eight-Nine asked. "All my power is going to my primary transmit antenna."

Three-Five quickly raised and lowered her front which consisted of two small turning blades, indicating she would.

"I'll find Six-Five. She's flying around the perimeter of our area again, once again, looking for changes in the landscape. I'll tell her and then the two of us can fly around and tell the others."

Eight-Nine made a chirp in agreement. The two flying robots were the best at spreading news to the rest of the robots, particularly the ones like Eight-Nine, that were completely immobile.

"Please ask One-Four to visit me," Eight-Nine added. "If Swell Driver is headed here, I'd like to work out a plan with One-Four that we can propose to Three. We have to figure out the right way to proceed and be clear about it."

Three-Five made her final gesture indicating she would do as asked and then flew away leaving Eight-Nine with her signals and the thoughts that bounced around her circuits. She was a little worried that maybe Swell Driver wasn't on his way and it was simply a signal with too many bit errors. If so, she'd be blamed for spinning everyone up.

But if not, Swell Driver, and any robot or robots that were with him, were going to find out things that no robot should ever know about their creators.

* * *

What's next for Ruby and her robot friends? Grab book four: *Eleven Little Robots*

A Word or Two From the Author

Thank you for reading *Silly Insane Humans!* I hope you enjoyed it and are looking forward to the final novel in the series! By 'final' I mean it will close out this 'trilogy in four parts,' if I may borrow a phrase from one of my own favorite sci-fi novel series. But that doesn't mean the adventures these characters have will be over…

The two people I have to thank most right now are 1) my hubby, for hopefully the obvious reason that the life of an author's spouse is never an easy one when you have continually have to share that life with the imaginary world said author is constantly thinking about and 2) my editor who still continues to remind me about human emotions and how to write them down.

To ensure you stay updated on book releases:

Join my mailing list at: https://adeenamignogna.com

With deepest appreciation,
Adeena

Silly Insane Humans

About Adeena

Adeena Mignogna is a physicist and astronomer (by degree) working in aerospace as a Mission Architect, which just means she's been doing it so long they had to give her a fun title. More importantly, she's a long-time science fiction geek with a strong desire to inspire others through speaking and writing about robots, aliens, artificial intelligence, computers, longevity, exoplanets, virtual reality, and more. She writes science fiction novels, to include The Robot Galaxy Series (available on Amazon) and loves spending time with her fellow co-hosts of The BIG Sci-Fi Podcast (available wherever you listen to podcasts)!

Adeena lives in Maryland, USA with her hubby, two kids, a pile of computers, one half-completed robot cat, two biological cats (Ruby and Pearl), and an ever-increasing collection of Silicon Dioxide from around planet Earth.

https://adeenamignogna.com

Silly Insane Humans

Printed in Great Britain
by Amazon

43886320R00138